ANNE

Adapted by DONALD HARRON

Music by NORMAN CAMPBELL

From the Novel by L. M. Montgomery

Lyrics by

DONALD HARRON *and*
NORMAN CAMPBELL

Additional Lyrics by

MAVOR MOORE *and*
ELAINE CAMPBELL

D1636510

SAMUEL FRENCH, INC.

45 WEST 25TH STREET   NEW YORK 10010
7623 SUNSET BOULEVARD HOLLYWOOD 90046
LONDON   TORONTO

Amateurs wishing to arrange for the production of ANNE OF GREEN GABLES must make application to SAMUEL FRENCH, INC. at 45 West 25th Street, New York, NY   10010, giving the following particulars:

    (1) The name of the town and theatre or hall in which it is proposed to give the production

    (2) The maximum seating capacity of the theatre or hall.

    (3) Scale of ticket prices.

    (4) The number of performances it is intended to give, and the dates thereof.

    (5) Indicate whether you will use an orchestration or simply a piano.

Upon receipt of these particulars SAMUEL FRENCH, INC., will quote the terms upon which permission for performances will be granted.

A standard rental package consisting of: Piano/Conductor's score, Flute/Piccolo, Oboes I & II, Bassoons I & II, Clarinet I, Clarinet II, Trumpet I, Trumpet II, Horn I, Horn II, Trombone, Percussion (Timpani, Vibraphone, Xylophone, Drums), Violin I, Violin II, Violin III, Viola, Cello, Bass, Harp, (no chorus books available), will be loaned two months prior to the production ONLY on receipt of the royalty quoted for all performances, the rental fee and a refundable deposit. The deposit will be refunded on the safe return to SAMUEL FRENCH, INC. of all material loaned for the production.

All Amateur and Stock Companies producing this work must accord billing credits as per the following:

ANNE OF GREEN GABLES
A Musical

Adapted by	*Music by*
DONALD HARRON	NORMAN CAMPBELL

From the Novel by L. M. Montgomery
Lyrics by DONALD HARRON *and* NORMAN CAMPBELL

Additional Lyrics by
MAVOR MOORE *and* ELAINE CAMPBELL

(Novel adapted by permission of the publishers,
Farrar, Straus & Giroux, Inc.)
Originally commissioned and presented by the
Charlottetown Festival, Canada

ANNE OF GREEN GABLES was presented at the City Center
55 Street Theater in December 1971. The Charlottetown Festival
Production was directed and choreographed by Alan Lund.
Adapted by Donald Harron from the novel by L. M. Montgomery,
the production was designed by Murray Laufer. The cast was as
follows:

CAST
(In Order of Appearance)

MRS. RACHEL LYNDE	*Maud Whitmore*
MRS. MACPHERSON	*Cleone Duncan*
MRS. BARRY	*Nancy Kerr*
MRS. SLOANE	*Flora MacKenzie*
MRS. PYE	*Kathryn Watt*
THE MINISTER	*Lloyd Malenfant*
EARL, the mailman	*Bill Hosie*
CECIL, the farmer	*George Merner*
MARILLA CUTHBERT	*Elizabeth Mawson*
MATTHEW CUTHBERT, her brother	*Peter Mews*
ANNE SHIRLEY	*Gracie Finley*
MRS. SPENCER	*Flora Mackenzie*
MRS. BLEWETT	*Roma Hearn*
DIANA BARRY	*Glenda Landry*

Young ladies at Avonlea School

PRISSY ANDREWS	*Sharlene McLean*
JOSIE PYE	*Barbara Barsky*
RUBY GILLIS	*Patti Toms*
TILLIE BOULTER	*Lynn Marsh*
GERTIE PYE	*Deborah Millar*

Boys at Avonlea School

GILBERT BLYTHE	*Jeff Hyslop*
CHARLIE SLOANE	*George Juriga*
MOODY MACPHERSON	*Dan Costain*
GERRY BUOTE	*Andre Denis*
TOMMY SLOANE	*John Powell*
MALCOLM ANDREWS	*Calvin McRae*
MR. PHILLIPS, the schoolmaster	*Jack Northmore*
LUCILLA, clerk in Blair's store	*Cleone Duncan*
MISS STACY, the schoolmistress	*Roma Hearn*
THE STATIONMASTER	*Bill Hosie*

The story is set in Avonlea, a tiny village in Prince Edward
Island, Canada's smallest province, at the turn of the Century.

5

MUSICAL NUMBERS

ACT ONE

1. "Great Workers for the Cause" .. *Rachel Lynde and Ladies*
2. "Where Is Matthew Going?" .... *The Townspeople*
3. "Gee I'm Glad I'm No One Else But Me" .... *Anne*
4. Trio: "We Clearly Requested" .. *Marilla, Anne, Matthew*
5. "The Facts" .. *Anne, Mrs. Spencer, Mrs. Blewett, Marilla*
6. "Where'd Marilla Come From?" (reprise) .... *Mailman, Farmer and Ladies*
7. "Humble Pie" .... *Matthew and Anne*
8. "Oh Mrs. Lynde!" .... *Anne*
9. "Back to School Ballet" .... *The Pupils*
10. "Avonlea, We Love Thee" ...... *Mr. Phillips and Pupils*
11. "Wondrin'" .... *Gilbert*
12. "Did You Hear?" .. *Josie, Mrs. Pye, Lucilla, Mrs. Barry, Mailman, Farmer, Mrs. Lynde*
13. "Ice Cream" .... *Diana and The Company*
14. "The Picnic" .... *The Company*

ACT TWO

1. "Where Did the Summer Go To?" .... *The Pupils*
2. "Kindred Spirits" .... *Anne and Diana*
3. "Open the Window!" .... *Miss Stacy and Pupils*
4. "The Words" .... *Matthew*
5. "Open the Window!" (reprise) ... *Miss Stacy and Pupils*
6. "Nature Hunt Ballet" .... *The Pupils*
7. "I'll Show Him" .... *Anne and Gilbert*
8. "General Store" .. *Lucilla, Matthew and the Townspeople*
9. "Pageant Song" .... *The Pupils*
10. "If It Hadn't Been for Me" .... *The Company*
11. "Where Did the Summer Go To?" (reprise) .. *Anne, Gilbert and the Pupils*
12. "Anne of Green Gables" .... *Matthew*
13. "The Words" (reprise) .... *Marilla*
14. "Wondrin'" (reprise) .... *Anne and Gilbert*

Anne of Green Gables

VOICES *are heard behind the dimly lighted flower scrim.*

OVERTURE.
ANNE OF GREEN GABLES, NEVER CHANGE,
WE LIKE YOU JUST THIS WAY.
ANNE OF GREEN GABLES, SWEET AND STRANGE,
STAY AS YOU ARE TODAY.

THOUGH BLOSSOMS FADE AND FRIENDS MUST
    PART,
OLD GROW THE SONGS WE'VE SUNG,
ANNE OF GREEN GABLES, IN OUR HEARTS,
YOU ARE FOREVER YOUNG.

(INSTRUMENTAL OVERTURE.)

ACT ONE

SCENE 1

FLOWER SCRIM.

LIGHTS UP. RACHEL LYNDE *is on her way to the weekly meeting of the Avonlea Ladies' Aid.* MRS. SLOANE *joins her, then* MRS. BARRY, *followed by* MRS. MACPHERSON, *and finally* MRS. PYE.

SONG: *"GREAT WORKERS FOR THE CAUSE"*

LADIES.
EVERY TUESDAY AFTERNOON,
WE TAKE UP OUR POSITIONS
IN THE RUMMAGE BRIGADE OF THE LADIES' AID
TO THE BOARD OF FOREIGN MISSIONS.
ALL THE LADIES OF AVONLEA
ARE GLAD TO HELP THE HEATHEN:
MRS. SLOANE.
TO IMPROVE THE LOT OF THE HOTTENTOT
COMES NATURAL TO US AS BREATHIN' . . .
LADIES.
AS NATURAL TO US AS BREATHIN'. . . .

WE ARE GREAT WORKERS FOR THE CAUSE,
WILLING HELPERS IN THE MISSION FIELDS:
WE DO EVERYTHING WE KIN DO—
MRS. PYE. (*Spoken.*) We send afghans to the Hindu!
LADIES.
WE ARE GREAT WORKERS FOR THE CAUSE.

WE'RE COLLECTING UNDERSHIRTS AND DRAWERS
FOR TO KEEP THE NAKED PAGANS WARM.
MRS. SLOANE.
WHEN YOUR CHILDREN GET TOO BIG WE
SEND THEIR UNDIES TO A PYGMY.
LADIES.
WE ARE ALL GREAT WORKERS FOR THE . . .

(*The song is interrupted by a scream from* RACHEL LYNDE.)

MRS. LYNDE. (*Staring out over audience.*) Oh! Look!! It's Matthew Cuthbert, driving a buggy, dressed like he was goin' to a funeral.

8

ALL. Matthew Cuthbert?
MRS. BARRY. Driving a buggy . . .
MRS. MACPHERSON. . . . in his Sunday suit . . .
MRS. PYE. . . . on a Tuesday?
MRS. SLOANE. Why isn't he home bugging his potatoes?
MRS. LYNDE. Yooooooo-ooooh, Matthew, where you off to?
MRS. MACPHERSON. He didn't say.
MRS. BARRY. Matthew never does.
MRS. PYE. That's the truth.

SONG: *"WHERE IS MATTHEW GOING?"*
(LADIES, FARMER, MAILMAN.)

LADIES.
WHERE IS MATTHEW GOING, AND WHY IS HE
    GOING THERE?
MATTHEW CUTHBERT NEVER, NEVER GOES
    ANYWHERE.
HE'S WEARING HIS CLEAN WHITE COLLAR.
HE'S WEARING HIS STORE-BOUGHT SUIT . . .
    MRS. MACPHERSON.
LET'S GET US A RIG AND FOLLER . . .
    MRS. BARRY.
DON'T BE SILLY . . .
    MRS. PYE.
DON'T BE SASSY . . .
    MRS. LYNDE.
DON'T BE CUTE!

(*Enter* FARMER *and* MAILMAN. *They also stare out front.*)

LADIES.
WHERE DO YOU S'POSE HE'S GOING?
HE'S HITCHED UP HIS SUNDAY STEED. . . .
    MEN.
HE SHOULD BE HOME A-SOWING,
A-SOWING TURNIP SEED.
    ALL.
IT MUST BE A FEARFUL TASK THEN,
IT MUST BE SOMETHING BAD.
    MRS. MACPHERSON.
WHY DON'T WE ALL GO AND ASK, THEN,
    MRS. BARRY.
ARE YOU BALMY?
    MRS. PYE.
ARE YOU BATTY?

MRS. LYNDE.
ARE YOU MAD?
ALL.
IF IT WAS BAD, HE'D DRIVE MUCH FASTER.
IF 'TWAS NUTHIN' HE'D DRIVE SLOW.
MRS. LYNDE.
I'D BETTER GO ASK HIS SISTER. . . .
ALL.
MARILLA'D BE SURE TO KNOW!
LADIES.
YOU'D BETTER GO ASK MARILLA,
YOU BETTER GO PAY A CALL.
MRS. LYNDE.
I'LL BORROW A DROP OF VANILLA
AND ACT SORT OF DUMB AND ALL!
ALL.
YOU CAN TALK ABOUT THE WEATHER,
THEN ASK HER ALL AT ONCE.
MRS. MACPHERSON.
WHY DON'T YOU ALL GO TOGETHER?
MRS. PYE.
WE'RE NO SNOOPERS!
MRS. BARRY.
WE'RE NO GOSSIPS!
MRS. LYNDE.
OH, YOU DUNCE!

(*Music suddenly stops when* MATTHEW'S *sister,* MARILLA CUTH-
BETH, *appears.*)

MARILLA. (*Enters.*) 'Afternoon, ladies. I'm late.
MRS. LYNDE. Why, Marilla Cuthbert, we thought you'd been
called to your maker when we saw your brother drive by in his
Sunday suit.
MRS. PYE. And on a Tuesday.
MRS. MACPHERSON. Matthew Cuthbert's so shy he's never
moved farther than from the house to the barn.
MARILLA. Matthew went to Bright River to meet the train.
ALL. The train?
MARILLA. We're getting a little boy from the orphanage in Nova
Scotia.
MRS. LYNDE. Well, you're never through with surprises 'til
you're dead.
MARILLA. We've been thinking about it ever since last harvest
when Matthew had the heart attack. You know how desperate

hard it's got to be to get hired help these days, and when Mrs. Alex Spencer told us she was going to adopt herself a little girl we decided to ask Mrs. Spencer to pick us out a boy while she was there. Old enough to be of some use in doing the heavy work and young enough to be trained up proper.

MRS. BARRY. But, Marilla, you don't really know what you are getting.

MRS. LYNDE. Now don't say I didn't warn you if this imported orphan puts strychnine in the well and burns your house to the ground. I heard of an orphan over in Nova Scotia did just that and the whole family died in fearful agonies. As I remember it was a girl in that instance.

MARILLA. You can stop saying your prayers on our account, Rachel, we're not getting a girl!

MRS. LYNDE. Well, I think it's a mighty risky thing you're doin', that's what!

MARILLA. There's risks in people having children of their own when it comes to that.

MRS. LYNDE. Well, it's hardly a risk in the case of you and your brother!

(Music resumes.)

LADIES.
OUR MEETING CAN CONTINUE,
NOW WE'VE FOUND OUT JUST WHERE . . .
    ALL.
WHERE THAT MATTHEW'S GOING
AND WHY HE'S GOING THERE!
    LADIES. *(March off singing:)*
WE ARE GREAT WORKERS FOR THE CAUSE
WILLING HELPERS IN THE MISSION FIELDS.

ACT ONE

SCENE 2

THE SIDE WALL OF THE BRIGHT RIVER R.R. STATION.

Sitting on a goods wagon is a GIRL *wearing an ugly brown dress and a faded sailor hat. Her hair is in two braids down her back. She holds on to a worn carpetbag with an air of tense expectation. She is waiting with all her might and main.*

As the light spreads further L. *to mid-stage,* MATTHEW CUTHBERT *appears, passes the* GIRL *sitting on the goods wagon. He is looking for the stationmaster. He looks everywhere. Eventually he becomes aware that someone is following him wherever he goes. It is the little* GIRL. MATTHEW *sidesteps her shyly, looks up and down the track and finally consults his watch.*

GIRL. (ANNE.) If you're looking for the five-thirty train it's been and gone.

MATTHEW. Oh.

ANNE. Half an hour ago.

MATTHEW. It's . . . uh . . . only twenty past five. (*Looks around some more.*)

ANNE. If you're looking for the stationmaster, he told me to tell you he's gone home.

MATTHEW. He told you . . . to tell me . . . ?

ANNE. I suppose you are Mr. Matthew Cuthbert. Mrs. Spencer told me what you looked like. I was beginning to be afraid you weren't coming for me. The stationmaster said the train was early because they had a new engineer on and he wasn't very experienced.

MATTHEW. There must be some mistake.

ANNE. Yes. He said usually the 5:30 train is half an hour late, regular as clockwork. If you hadn't come for me I was going to walk down the track to that big wild cherry tree. . . . See it? (*Points. He looks obediently.*)

MATTHEW. Oh yes.

ANNE. And I was going to climb into that beautiful tree and stay all night. Wouldn't that be lovely? Am I talking too much? People are always telling me I do. Mrs. Spencer said my tongue must be hung in the middle, it flaps so. If you say so, I'll stop. I c*an* stop when I make up my mind, although it's awfully difficult.

MATTHEW. No, you can talk all you want. I don't mind.

ANNE. Oh, I'm so glad. It seems so wonderful that I'm going to live with you and belong to you.

MATTHEW. I'll let Marilla do it.

ANNE. I beg your pardon ?

MATTHEW. Oh . . . ah . . . let me help you with your bag.

ANNE. Oh, I can carry it. It isn't heavy. It's an excruciatingly old bag. Thank goodness I'll never have to use it again. Mr. Cuthbert, which would you rather be if you had your wish? Divinely beautiful? or dazzlingly clever? or angelically good?

MATTHEW. Well now, I don't rightly know. (*Exits.*)

ANNE. Oh, neither do I. But it would be nice to think you had a choice. (*Exits.*)

(*DROP CURTAIN.* ANNE *and* MATTHEW *reappear riding in a buggy.* [*Horse optional.*] *It crosses the stage during the course of the song.*)

SONG: *"GEE I'M GLAD I'M NO ONE ELSE BUT ME"*

ANNE.
ONCE I THOUGHT I'D LIKE TO BE
A BLOSSOM GROWING ON A TREE,
WHITE AND PINK AND LAZY AS CAN BE.
BUT I'D BE KING JUST IN THE SPRING.
SO NOW I THINK IT OVER,
GEE I'M GLAD I'M NO ONE ELSE BUT ME.

IF YOU SIT AROUND AND FIND THE WORLD IS
     GLOOMY
AND IT ISN'T JUST YOUR CUP OF TEA
IT'S EASY TO IMAGINE THAT IT'S ROSE-IN-BLOOMY,
YOU CAN THINK THE THINGS YOU WANT TO BE.

SO WHEN ALL IS SAID AND DONE
IMAGINING'S A LOT OF FUN,
BUT WHEN THERE ARE BATTLES TO BE WON
BE WHAT YOU ARE, IT'S BEST BY FAR
AND SOON YOU'LL BE IN CLOVER.
GEE, I'M GLAD I'M NO ONE ELSE BUT ME!

Mr. Cuthbert!
     MATTHEW. (*Pulls on the reins, the buggy stops.*) Ho, Pearl!
     ANNE. Your roads! They're red! Oh, I'm so sorry!
     MATTHEW. Don't you like them?
     ANNE. Mr. Cuthbert, what color would you say this is?
     MATTHEW. Why, it's red, ain't it?
     ANNE. Yes. Red hair and freckles have been my lifelong sorrows. But why are your roads red?
     MATTHEW. Well now . . . I remember a fellow telling me once it was the iron in the soil getting rusty. But I don't think he could have meant it.
     ANNE.
DO YOU SUPPOSE THAT IT COULD BE
THE WOUNDS OF TRAGIC DESTINY
DRIPPING FROM A BLOODSTAINED FAMILY TREE?

AN EVIL SPELL THAT DID COMPEL
THE FOUNDERS OF THIS ISLAND
TO MEET THEIR DOOM AND PERISH HORRIBLY.

PICTURE NOW THE VICIOUS STRIFE THAT
        STARTED RAGING
WAY BACK IN THE OLDEN DAYS OF YORE . . .
FAMILY WITH FAMILY IN FEUDS ENGAGING,
DRENCHING ALL YOUR LOCAL SOIL WITH GORE!

THERE! AS FAR AS I CAN SEE
I'VE JUST CLEARED UP THE MYSTERY
OF WHY YOUR ROADS ARE RED PERPETUALLY!
    MATTHEW.
THE ANSWER'S FOUND
NOT IN THE GROUND . . .
IN YOUR IMAGINATION!

Gee up, Pearl!

(Buggy starts again.)

    ANNE.
GEE, I'M GLAD I'M NO ONE ELSE!
GEE, I'M GLAD I'M NO ONE ELSE!
GEE, I'M GLAD I'M NO ONE ELSE BUT ME!

(Buggy disappears off stage.)

ACT ONE

SCENE 3

THE HOUSE AT GREEN GABLES.

Enter MATTHEW *and* ANNE. MATTHEW *hesitates, takes a deep breath.*

    MATTHEW. You come right on in.
    MARILLA. (*Upstairs in the bedroom.*) Matthew?
    MATTHEW. Yes, Marilla.

(MARILLA *comes downstairs.*)

MARILLA. Why, Matthew Cuthbert!

MATTHEW. Yes.

MARILLA. Who's that?

MATTHEW. Eh?

MARILLA. Where's the boy?

MATTHEW. Oh well . . . well now, there wasn't any boy. There was only . . . her.

MARILLA. There must have been a boy. We sent word to Mrs. Spencer to bring us a boy.

MATTHEW. Well, she didn't. She brought her.

MARILLA. This is a pretty piece of business!

ANNE. (*Slamming down the suitcase.*) You don't want me! You don't want me because I'm not a boy! Oh, I might have known it! (*Sits in a slump at the table.*)

MATTHEW. I got to water the mare. (*Exits.*)

MARILLA. There, there, child, there's no need to cry so!

ANNE. There *is* need! This is the most tragic thing that has ever happened to me!

MARILLA. Well, we're not going to throw you out of doors, tonight at any rate. Now what's your name?

ANNE. Would you please call me Cordelia?

MARILLA. *Call* you Cordelia? Is that your name?

ANNE. Well no, it's not exactly my name . . . actually it's Anne. Anne Shirley, but whenever I'm in dire anguish, I've always imagined that my name is Cordelia. At least I always have of late years.

MARILLA. Fiddlesticks! If your name is Anne, that's what you should be called. It's a good plain sensible name, you've no need to be ashamed of it.

ANNE. Well, if you call me Anne, would you please call me Anne spelled with an "e"?

MARILLA. What difference does it make how it's spelled?

ANNE. Oh, it *looks* so much nicer.

MARILLA. Very well, then, Anne with an "e," can you tell me how this mistake came to be made? We sent word to Mrs. Spencer to bring us a boy. Were there no boys at the orphanage?

ANNE. Oh yes, an abundance. But I distinctly heard Mrs. Spencer say that you wanted a girl, and the matron said she thought I'd do.

MARILLA. A girl would be of no use to us! We want a boy to help Matthew on the farm. Take your hat off over there. And help me with the table; we'll have supper.

ANNE. Oh, I couldn't eat. I'm in the depths of despair. Can you eat when you're in the depths of despair?

MARILLA. I don't know. I've never been there so I can't say.

MATTHEW. (*Entering.*) She's tired, Marilla. Best put her to bed.

MARILLA. Very well, child, bring your bag and come with me.

MATTHEW. Good night.

ANNE. How can you say it's a good night when you know it must be the very worst night I've ever had! My life is a perfect graveyard of broken hopes. (*Follows* MARILLA *upstairs.*)

MARILLA. What was that!

ANNE. That's a sentence I read in a book once and I say it to myself whenever I'm disappointed in anything.

MARILLA. You can sleep in here.

ANNE. (*Flops on the bed and stares out of the window.*) . . . OOOOOOOH!

MARILLA. Mercy, child, what's the matter?

ANNE. A tree of your very own! Imagine!

MARILLA. It's a big tree and it blooms great, but the cherries don't amount to much. Small and wormy.

ANNE. Snow Queen.

MARILLA. What?

ANNE. I'll call the tree Snow Queen, because it reminds me of the blinding vision of the White Way of Delight.

MARILLA. You've got a tongue in your head, that's for certain. Now I want you to get undressed.

ANNE. I have my best underwear on. The matron said you never know when you might get cut up in a train wreck.

MARILLA. (*Looking in the suitcase.*) I suppose you have a nightgown?

ANNE. I have two.

MARILLA. They look kinda flimsy. You'd best wear both of them. After you're undressed I want you to say your prayers.

ANNE. Oh, I never say any prayers.

MARILLA. Don't you know who God is?

ANNE. The matron at the orphanage told me that God is the one who made my hair red and I've never cared about Him since.

MARILLA. I'm afraid you're a very wicked little girl to talk this way. This is a Christian house and while you're in it you'll say your prayers. And when you've finished, I want you to blow out the candle. No, on second thought I'd best wait here 'til you're done. You're liable to set the house on fire.

ANNE. You may take the candle. After I'm in bed I'll imagine out a nice prayer to say.

MARILLA. No, no, child. You must kneel by your bed to pray to your Maker.

ANNE. (*Kneels.*) I'm ready. What do I say?

MARILLA. Uh . . . ah . . . now I lay me down to sleep . . . You'd best talk to the Lord in your own words, child.

ANNE. (*Her voice getting deeper in tone.*) I'll do my best. "Gracious heavenly Father, infinite, eternal and unchangeable . . ."

MARILLA. Mercy on us, what was that?

ANNE. That's the way the minister who came to the orphanage used to do it.

MARILLA. Stop your chattering and get on with your prayers. And use your own words.

ANNE. My dear God . . . Oh, Miss Cuthbert, even though I'm not going to stay here at Green Gables, I think I could make a much nicer prayer if I imagined that I am.

MARILLA. Never mind your imaginings. Just thank Him humbly for the blessings He has given.

ANNE. That's where I *need* my imagination!

Dear God,
Thank you for the White Way of Delight
and the Snow Queen.
I'm really extremely grateful for them.
And that's all the blessings I can think of just now
to thank You for.
As for the things I want
it would take a great deal of time to mention them all,
so I'll only name the two most important:
Please let me stay at Green Gables,
And *please* let me be good-looking when I grow up.

I remain,
Yours respectfully,
Anne Shirley.

There, did I do it alright? I could have made it much more flowery if I'd had time to think it over!

MARILLA. Go to sleep now.

ANNE. Oh, I just thought. I should have said "Amen" in place of "yours respectfully," the way the ministers do. Do you suppose it will make any difference?

MARILLA. I don't suppose so. Now go to sleep. (*Goes downstairs.* MATTHEW *is waiting in the rocking chair.*) This is what comes of sending someone instead of going ourselves. One of us will have to drive over to Mrs. Spencer's tomorrow, that's for certain. The child will have to go back to the orphanage.

MATTHEW. Yes, I suppose so.

MARILLA. You suppose so? Don't you know it?

MATTHEW. Well, now, she's a nice little thing, Marilla. It seems kind of a pity to send her back when she's so set on staying.

MARILLA. Matthew Cuthbert! You don't mean to say you think we ought to keep her! What good would she be to us?

MATTHEW. We might be some good to her.

MARILLA. I never *heard* of such a thing. She'll have to be dispatched straightaway back to where she came from.

MATTHEW. Well now, I could maybe hire a boy to help me . . . and she'd be company for you. She's a real interesting little thing.

MARILLA. I'm not suffering for company. . . . I believe that child has you bewitched! I can see plain as plain that you want to keep her.

MATTHEW. You should have heard her talk coming from the station.

MARILLA. Oh, she can talk. I saw that straightaway. It's nothing in her favor either. I don't like children who have so much to say. I don't *want* an orphan girl, and if I did she isn't the style I'd pick out. We're not going to keep her, so you might as well spare your breath to cool your porridge.

MATTHEW. (*Rising from table.*) Well now, it's just as you say, of course, Marilla.

MARILLA. Where are you gadding off to? You haven't touched a bite of your supper.

MATTHEW. I don't suppose I'm hungry either. (*Picks up lantern and exits.*)

MARILLA. How could Mrs. Spencer have made such a mistake?

SONG: *"WE CLEARLY REQUESTED A BOY"*

MARILLA, MATTHEW *and* ANNE.
WE CLEARLY REQUESTED A BOY!
MATTHEW.
A BOY'S WHAT WE WANTED, I GUESS.
ANNE.
I GUESS THAT A GIRL'S NOT SO BAD.
MARILLA.
SO BADLY WE NEEDED A *BOY,*
WE CLEARLY REQUESTED A BOY.
ANNE.
A BOY'S WHAT THEY WANTED, I GUESS. . . .
MATTHEW.
I GUESS THAT A GIRL'S NOT SO BAD.

MARILLA.
SO BADLY WE NEEDED A BOY.
ANNE.
A BOY COULD HELP OUT ON THE FARM. . . .
MATTHEW.
THE FARM COULD LOOK AFTER ITSELF. . . .
ANNE.
IT'S SELFISH TO THINK OF MYSELF!
MARILLA.
MYSELF I AM PARTIAL TO BOYS. . . .
MATTHEW.
BOYS. . . .
ANNE.
BOYS!!!
MATTHEW.
A GIRL COULD HELP MARILLA ROUND THE HOUSE,
A GIRL COULD BRING ALFALFA TO THE COWS.
MARILLA.
A BOY CAN MILK AND CARRY IN THE PAILS.
ANNE.
BOYS ARE MADE OF SNAILS AND PUPPY DOG
      TAILS!
MARILLA.
A BOY CAN PLOW, A BOY CAN HAY AND HOE,
A GIRL CAN ONLY SIT AND KNIT AND SEW.
MATTHEW.
A BOY IS ROUGH BUT GIRLS ARE STILL AS MICE.
ANNE.
GIRLS ARE MADE OF SPICE. . . . OH, WON'T THEY
      THINK TWICE?
SHE HATES ME BECAUSE I'M A GIRL. . . .
MATTHEW.
A GIRL IS ALRIGHT, I DECLARE . . . .
MARILLA.
I DECLARE THAT SHE'LL HAVE TO GO BACK!
ANNE.
GO BACK.
MARILLA.
GO BACK.
MATTHEW.
GO BACK.
MARILLA.
WE CLEARLY REQUESTED
ANNE.
LIKE ALL OF THE REST DID.

MATTHEW.
IT CAN'T BE CONTESTED.
ALL THREE.
WE (THEY) CLEARLY REQUESTED A BOY.

(ANNE *blows out the candle.*)

BLACKOUT

ACT ONE

SCENE 4

PATCH QUILT DROP.

MRS. SPENCER *checking the contents of her bag. Enter* MARILLA.

MRS. SPENCER. Marilla Cuthbert! What a surprise! What
brings you our way?
MARILLA. The fact is, Mrs. Spencer, that when we asked . . .
MRS. SPENCER. Is that little Anne sitting out there in the
buggy? Isn't she the dear wee thing!
MARILLA. The fact is, Mrs. Spencer, there's been some sort of
queer mistake somewhere. We sent word through your brother
Robert for you to bring us a boy.
MRS. SPENCER. You don't tell me! Isn't that funny? How did
that happen, I wonder? I'm dreadful sorry, Marilla, I thought
I was following your instructions. Isn't it a funny predicament!
Ha, ha, ha.
MARILLA. The thing to do now, Mrs. Spencer, is to put it
right. I suppose the orphanage will take the child back?
MRS. SPENCER. Mrs. Peter Blewett. The very thing! I don't
think we'll have to send the child back to Nova Scotia. You just
come along with me right now. I always say it's an ill wind that
doesn't blow somebody into town.

(They exit.)

ACT ONE

SCENE 5

MRS. BLEWETT'S HOUSE.

A ramshackle little place full of washing hanging up to dry.

Enter MRS. SPENCER *followed by* MARILLA *and* ANNE.

MRS. SPENCER. Yoohooo, Mrs. Blewett.

MRS. BLEWETT. C'min.

MRS. SPENCER. Lovely to see you again. My, what a dear little home you have. May I introduce my friend, Miss Marilla Cuthbert?

MRS. BLEWETT. Howdoo.

MARILLA. Mrs. Blewett.

MRS. SPENCER. And this dear little girl. You remember that little matter we spoke of last week?

MRS. BLEWETT. She available?

MRS. SPENCER. Yes, and I know you and she could become firm friends.

(CHILDREN *are heard crying offstage.*)

MRS. BLEWETT. Them kids . . . I keep 'em in the woodshed till feeding time. (*To* ANNE.) Here, you! Go stir the stew. All right, I'm comin' out there and whale the daylights out of you! (*Exits.*)

MRS. SPENCER. The good Lord has seen fit to reward her labors. She's had twins three times in a row.

MARILLA. How many children in all?

MRS. SPENCER. Seven . . . (*Sound cue: BABY CRY.*) no . . . eight.

MARILLA. She'd be a Roman Catholic?

MRS. SPENCER. No, Presbyterian.

MARILLA. How long has she been married?

MRS. SPENCER. Five years . . . going on six.

MARILLA. Funny kind of Presbyterian.

MRS. BLEWETT. (*Re-enters.*) Dinner's coming! Just sit out there and suck your fingers. All right, you, what's your name?

SONG: *"THE FACTS"*

ANNE.

I'M THE LADY CORDELIA DE MONTMORENCY
ABDUCTED BY GYPSIES WHEN I WAS THREE . . .

MARILLA. Anne!

ANNE. My name is Anne Shirley. Anne with an "e."

MRS. BLEWETT. That's better; just the facts.

MRS. SPENCER. Tell her where you were born and who your folks were.

ANNE.

I WAS BORN IN A PALACE IN OLD VIENNA,
DANUBIAN WALTZES MY LULLABIES:
MY FATHER WAS JOHANN WITH GREAT
    MUSTACHES,
MY MOTHER MARIA WITH EMERALD EYES.

MRS. BLEWETT. Where did you say you was born?

ANNE.

MY DEAR PARENTS WERE RICH AND
    ARISTOCRATIC
WITH TEN MAIDS AND BUTLERS TO BRING YOU
    TEA:
AND WE'D RIDE IN A CARRIAGE WITH FOOTMEN
    ON IT
AND ALL OF THEM CURTSIED AND BOWED TO ME!

MARILLA. That's enough of that, child!

ANNE.

IF YOU'RE WONDERING HOW I GOT *HERE*
I WAS KIDNAPED BY THIS BUCCANEER,
WHO TOOK ME TO FRANCE
AND TAUGHT ME TO DANCE
IN HIS GYPSY HIDEOUT IN TANGIER!

(ANNE *does a wild gypsy dance around the room. Everyone is
    aghast.* MARILLA *finally grabs hold of her.*)

MARILLA. Anne, stop it this instant!

MRS. SPENCER. I never heard such nonsense in all my life!

MRS. BLEWETT. I don't think the girl's all there!

MRS. SPENCER. That's certainly not what they told me at the orphanage!

MARILLA. Anne! Anne Shirley!

MRS. BLEWETT. We don't want no gypsies around here!

MRS. SPENCER. Whatever possessed that child?

MARILLA. Anne Shirley, just where do you think you are?

MRS. BLEWETT. And who do you think you are?

ANNE.

I'M THE LADY CORDELIA DE MONTMORENCY
ABDUCTED BY GYPSIES WHEN I WAS THREE . . .

MRS. BLEWETT, MRS. SPENCER and MARILLA.
THE FACTS, THE FACTS, THE FACTS,
THE PLAIN SIMPLE HOMELY UNEMBROIDERED
    FACTS.

MRS. SPENCER. Here! Here are the facts! *This* is the report they gave me at the orphanage: Name, Anne Shirley . . .

ANNE. Spelled with an "e."

MRS. SPENCER. Parents, deceased. Father, Walter Shirley, teacher of agriculture and rapid calculation at Bolingbroke Continuation School. Mother, Bertha Shirley, housewife.

ANNE. I have to imagine what they looked like. I was only three months old when they died.

MRS. SPENCER. Never mind, dear, you're going to have a new home now. What you lose on the sauce, you gain on the gander. Now where was I? Temporary Guardian, Mrs. Russell Thomas . . .

ANNE. And her drunken husband.

MRS. SPENCER. Oh, dear, that's not a nice thing to say!

ANNE. It's not a very nice thing to watch either! But then they sent me up the river. . . .

MARILLA. Up the river?

ANNE. To Mrs. Hammond and her five children.

MRS. BLEWETT. Good. Then you've had experience.

ANNE. Yes, I have, thank you.

SO, I LIVED WITH THE THOMASES THEN THE
    HAMMONDS,
I LIVED WITH A FAMILY IN HALIFAX,
BUT NONE OF THEM WANTED ME SO I WENT
    TO THE
HOME FOR THE ORPHANS AND THOSE ARE THE
    FACTS.

MRS. BLEWETT. Are you sure?

MRS. SPENCER. Yes, it's all written down here.

ANNE.
THE PLAIN SIMPLE HOMELY UNEMBROIDERED
    FACTS.

MRS. BLEWETT. Well, turn around—there ain't much of you, but what there is, is wiry. I'll expect you to earn your keep . . . all right, Mrs. Spencer, I'll take her.

MARILLA. Well, I don't know. I just came over to find out from Mrs. Spencer how the mistake had occurred. I feel I oughtn't to decide anything without consulting my brother. I think I'd best take the child home again and talk it over with him.

MRS. BLEWETT. But I thought . . .

MARILLA. If we decide not to keep her, I'll bring her back tomorrow night. Will that suit you, Mrs. Blewett?

MRS. BLEWETT. I s'pose it'll have to.

MRS. SPENCER. Well, we'll just leave it at that, then. We'll just put off till tomorrow instead of burning our bridges today.

(MARILLA *takes* ANNE *by the hand and leads her out, followed by* MRS. SPENCER.)

ACT ONE

SCENE 6

PATCH QUILT DROP.

FARMER *is hoeing.* MAILMAN *crosses.*

MAILMAN. 'Mornin', Cecil.

FARMER. 'Mornin', Earl. Any mail?

MAILMAN. Nothin' today, Cecil. Water's pretty choppy this mornin'. Mailboat didn't make it across.

FARMER. Isn't that a caution! The mainland's been cut off again.

MAILMAN. Where'd that buggy come from?

FARMER. I don't know, but it's headin' into Cuthberts'.

SONG: *"WHERE'D MARILLA COME FROM?"*
(MAILMAN, FARMER *and* LADIES.)

MAILMAN and FARMER.
WHERE'D MARILLA COME FROM?
SHE'S COMIN' UP FROM THE SOUTH. . . .
THE HORSE'S EYES ARE ROLLING,
HE'S FOAMING AT THE MOUTH!

WHOEVER IT IS SHE'S RACING
I CAN'T SEE HIM FOR DUST,
SHE'S DRIVING TO BEAT THE DEVIL.
FARMER. Like a cyclone!
MAILMAN. Like a whirlwind!
BOTH. Fit to bust!

(*Enter* MRS. BARRY *and* MRS. PYE.)

FARMER, MAILMAN, MRS. MACPHERSON, MRS. PYE and MRS. BARRY.

WHERE'D MARILLA COME FROM,
AND WHAT DID SHE HAVE IN THERE?
WHATEVER IT WAS HAD FRECKLES
AND HANKS OF LONG RED HAIR.

SHE COULDN'T DRIVE MUCH FASTER,
IT MUST BE SOMETHING DIRE!
MUST BE SOME DISASTER!
   FARMER.
IT'S A ROBBERY!
   MAILMAN.
IT'S A FIRE!
   MRS. MACPHERSON.
IT'S A . . .
   MRS. PYE.
IT'S A . . .
   FARMER.
SHE'S IN TROUBLE.
   MAILMAN.
IN A WHIRL.
   ALL.
IT'S AN ACCIDENT . . .
   MRS. SPENCER. (*Entering.*)
IT'S A GIRL!

(*They follow her out bursting with curiosity.*)

ACT ONE

SCENE 7

GREEN GABLES.

MARILLA. Take off your hat, help me with the table. Matthew should be in from chores any minute now.

ANNE. Oh please, Miss Cuthbert, won't you tell me if you're going to keep me or not? I tried to be patient all the way back in the buggy, but I really can't bear not knowing any longer.

MARILLA. Take this cloth and clean off the table.

ANNE. And then you'll tell me?

MARILLA. First I want you to go to the shed out back and get some sticks of wood for the stove.

ANNE. And that's when you'll tell me?

MARILLA. Hurry along out to the woodshed, child . . . and not too big sticks, mind!

(ANNE *exits. A moment later* MATTHEW *enters from the barn. Scrapes his boots. Enters.*)

MATTHEW. You're back.

MARILLA. So it would appear.

MATTHEW. I . . . I watered Pearl. She's having her oats now . . . we're getting a bit low on oats. I'd best drive over to Carmody or White Sands tomorrow. . . . Marilla, I still think that we . . . (*Turns, sees* ANNE *standing in the doorway.*)

MARILLA. Matthew! Mind the eggs! (MARILLA *takes pail of eggs from him. Exits.* ANNE *and* MATTHEW *do a dance of joy with the dinner plates until* MARILLA *re-enters.*) Matthew Cuthbert! What would Dr. Malcolm say? Have you no thought for your heart?

MATTHEW. You . . . you tell old Malcolm my heart's . . . never been better!

MARILLA. You sit down this minute or you'll get the heaves! (ANNE *looks at* MATTHEW. *Both do half a step but* MARILLA *cuts them off sharply.*) Now stop it. The both of you. I have something to say, although the Lord knows there's not much need to put it into words. Matthew and I . . . have decided . . . to keep you. That is, if you'll try to be a good little girl and help Matthew on the farm. (ANNE *cries.*) Mercy, child, why are you crying?

ANNE. I don't know why I'm crying. I'm so glad! Oh, glad doesn't seem to be the right word at all . . . it's much more than that. . . .

MARILLA. Well, when you find the right word we'll have supper.

(RACHEL LYNDE *knocks at screen door.*)

MATTHEW. Oh! I know who that is.

MARILLA. Come in, Rachel.

MRS. LYNDE. I saw you driving by in the buggy, so I thought I'd come over. Whatever happened to the boy?

MATTHEW. We . . . changed his mind . . . *her* mind . . . well, what I mean is . . . well . . . we wanted a girl, so we . . . got one. . . .

MARILLA. Anne, this is Mrs. Lynde come to see you. Isn't that nice of her?

MRS. LYNDE. I could tell by the pigtails flying by in the buggy you hadn't got what you expected. Well, well, well, they didn't pick you out for your looks, that's sure and certain. Come over here, let me have a look at you. Did you ever see such freckles, and hair as red as carrots!

ANNE. How dare you call me ugly? How dare you say I'm freckled and red-headed!

MARILLA. Anne!

ANNE. How would you like to have such things said about you? How would you like to be told that you are fat and dilapidated and probably hadn't a spark of imagination in you? Oh, I don't care if I hurt your feelings by saying so! I hope I do hurt them. You've hurt mine worse than they've ever been hurt before. And I'll never forgive you for it, never, never, NEVER!

MRS. LYNDE. Did you ever see such a temper?

MARILLA. Anne, you will apologize to Mrs. Lynde at once, and ask her to forgive you.

ANNE. I could never do that! I'm sorry I vexed *you*, Miss Cuthbert, but I'm glad I said what I just said. It gave me great satisfaction.

MRS. LYNDE. Well!!!!

MARILLA. You will go straight upstairs to your room and stay there until you're willing to apologize.

(ANNE *stomps upstairs.*)

MRS. LYNDE. You've taken on quite a responsibility there, Marilla. I don't envy anyone who has to bring *that* up!

MARILLA. You shouldn't have twitted her about her looks, Rachel.

MRS. LYNDE. You don't mean to tell me you're upholding that terrible display of temper?

MARILLA. I'm not trying to excuse her, but we must make allowances. She's never been taught what is right. And you *were* hard on her.

MRS. LYNDE. Well, I can see I'll have to be careful what I say around here in future, since the fine feelings of orphans, brought from goodness knows where, have to be given first consideration. (*Starts to exit.*)

MARILLA. You haven't had your tea, Rachel. (MRS. LYNDE *hesitates. Then she sits down.*) We'll just sit here and wait till Anne is willing to apologize.

MRS. LYNDE. If you take my advice . . . me, who's brought up ten children and buried two . . . you won't wait for anything. You'll go right outside and cut yourself a good-sized birch switch!

(MATTHEW *is starting to climb the stairs. His boots squeak.*)

MARILLA. Where you off to?

MATTHEW. Hmmm? Oh, well now, I just thought I'd . . . I'd . . .

MARILLA. Go upstairs?

MATTHEW. Yes!

MARILLA. You haven't been upstairs in this house since you helped me paper the spare room four years ago.

MATTHEW. I know. I just thought I'd take a look at it.

MARILLA. Mind what the doctor said about climbing stairs.

MATTHEW. Uh-huh.

MARILLA. Matthew! Don't you go interfering. Perhaps an old maid doesn't know much about disciplining children, but I guess she knows as much as an old bachelor. Cup of tea, Matthew?

MATTHEW. No, no, thank you, I think I'll just . . . (*Picks up pail of eggs.*) Oh, no! I think I'll go fill the cistern. (*Puts eggs down. Exits.*)

MARILLA. Well, Rachel, as long as you're here, I might as well show you the patchwork pieces I've been saving for the afghans we're making for the Borneo Head Hunters.

(MATTHEW *reappears outside house carrying a ladder.*)

MATTHEW. Anne . . . Anne . . . Lady Cordelia de Montmorency! Don't you think you'd better get this thing off your chest and get it over with?

ANNE. Oh, I couldn't, Matthew! You can lock me up in a damp dark dungeon inhabited by snakes and toads.

MATTHEW. Well, now, we're not in the habit of doing that. Come on down; Marilla's dreadful determined, you know. You're gonna have to say you're sorry sooner or later.

ANNE. (*Scrambling down ladder.*) She hadn't any right to call me ugly and red-headed.

MATTHEW. I heard you say as much yourself, only yesterday.

ANNE. But there's such a difference between saying a thing yourself and hearing someone else say it.

MATTHEW. (*Sits her up on a fence post.*) Anne, you listen to me . . .

SONG: *"HUMBLE PIE"*
(MATTHEW *and* ANNE.)

MATTHEW.
NEVER MIND HOW FOLKS TALK,
LET THEM ALL STRUT AND SQUAWK,
WHEN THEY CRITICIZE JUST PASS THEM BY.

IF THEY DO CARP AT YOU
DON'T GET UPSET,
FUSS, FUME OR FRET, OR GET INDIGESTION.
CRITICS CAN'T BOTHER ME,
'CAUSE I TELL THEM I AGREE,
IF THEY'RE FINDING FAULT I DON'T DENY . . .
YOU CAN DO IT IF YOU TRY,
YOU WON'T RUE IT, BE LIKE I,
I KEEP HAPPY EATING HUMBLE PIE.
 ANNE and MATTHEW.
HUMBLE PIE, HUMBLE PIE,
WE CAN EAT IT, YOU AND I,
THOUGH THE WORLD AROUND US MAY BE PROUD.
 MATTHEW.
NEVER MIND, YOU WILL FIND
THEY HAVE NO FIGHT,
 ANNE.
IF YOU'RE POLITE,
 MATTHEW.
THAT'S RIGHT,
 ANNE.
AND ANSWER THEIR QUESTIONS,
 ANNE and MATTHEW.
WITH A SMILE ALL THE WHILE,
TRY TO WALK THAT SECOND MILE.
TURN THE OTHER CHEEK AGAINST THE CROWD.
 MATTHEW.
YOU CAN DO IT, JUST YOU TRY IT.
WHY NOT TRY MY STEADY DIET?
 ANNE and MATTHEW.
WE'LL BE HAPPY EATING HUMBLE PIE.

(*DANCE.*)

MATTHEW. Can you do this step? (MATTHEW *does his version of a Highland fling.*)

ANNE. (*Imitating him.*) Yes!

MATTHEW. Very good, and how about this one?

ANNE. No!

MARILLA'S VOICE. (*Comes from the kitchen.*) Matthew, what's going on out there?

MATTHEW. Quick! Up the ladder!

YOU CAN DO IT, JUST YOU TRY IT.
WHY NOT TRY MY STEADY DIET?
 ANNE and MATTHEW.
WE'LL BE HAPPY EATING HUMBLE PIE.

(MATTHEW *and the ladder disappear as* MARILLA *reaches the top
   of the stairs.*)

MARILLA. Mercy, child, what are you doing there?
ANNE. (*In prayer at the foot of her bed.*) I have been wrestling
with my soul. And now I'm ready to go and tell Mrs. Lynde I'm
sorry I lost my temper.
MARILLA. Very well. Come with me. (*MUSIC: Funeral March
as* ANNE *and* MARILLA *descend the stairs.*) Matthew!
MATTHEW. Yes?
MARILLA. Matthew, come in here.
MATTHEW. (*Still breathing hard.*) All right.
MARILLA. I want you to see what a little discipline can do.

(ANNE *approaches* MRS. LYNDE. *She is well aware of the grandeur
   of the occasion.*)

SONG: *"OH MRS. LYNDE (APOLOGY)"*

ANNE.
MRS. LYNDE, OH, MRS. LYNDE,
YOU HAVE BEEN WRONGED AND I HAVE SINNED.
MY VERY SOUL IS SO CHAGRINED,
I ACTED SO UNDISCIPLINED!
I SHOULD HAVE LAUGHED, I SHOULD HAVE
      GRINNED,
I SHOULD HAVE BEEN MORE THICKER-SKINNED,
FORGIVE ME PLEASE, MY HOPES ARE PINNED
ON MRS. LYNDE.
MRS. LYNDE. Well now, I think that's very nicely done. . . .

(*But* ANNE *is not finished yet.*)

ANNE.
MY PUNISHMENT WAS NECESSARY . . .
UPSTAIRS JUST NOW IN SOLITARY . . .
I HAVE A TEMPER WHICH IS SCARY . . .
I KNOW I HAVE AND I'LL BE WARY . . .
YOU'LL FIND MY CONDUCT SALUTARY. . . .

I DON'T DESERVE THE HUMAN RACE,
JUST MAKE MY HEADSTONE COMMONPLACE
AND PRINT MY NAME IN LOWER CASE,
WITHOUT AN "E" . . . JUST LEAVE A SPACE . . .
PLEASE, MRS. LYNDE, YOUR RAGE RESCIND . . .
I'M OUT OF WIND! PLEASE . . . MRS. . . . LYNDE!

(MRS. LYNDE, *deeply moved, exits sobbing.* ANNE *collapses.* MATTHEW *catches her.*)

ACT ONE

SCENE 8

PATCH QUILT.

Enter MRS. BARRY *and her daughter,* DIANA.

MRS. BARRY. We'll wait here in the lane, Diana. Marilla will bring the child from the house.

DIANA. Oh, Mother, I'm dying to see what she's like.

MRS. BARRY. You must remember, dear, that this child is most unfortunate. She doesn't have a father or a mother, so you mustn't flaunt your own too much. It's not polite to talk to other children about things they themselves don't possess.

(*Enter* MARILLA *with* ANNE.)

MARILLA. Good morning, Mizz Barry, Diana. This is Anne.

MRS. BARRY. How are you, Anne?

ANNE. Thank you, ma'am, I'm as well as can be expected.

DIANA. Hello, Anne!

ANNE. Hello! You have a perfectly lovely name. Diana is my favorite heathen goddess.

MARILLA. Diana is a very nice little girl and her mother is very particular about who she plays with. Now, you don't want to keep her late for school. Here's your note for Mr. Phillips. I'll just slip over to your house if I may, Mizz Barry, and borrow that dress pattern you were telling me about. . . .

MRS. BARRY. Very well, Marilla. Mind you behave yourself now, Diana. Good-bye, dear.

DIANA. G'bye. . . . Oh, Mother? Do you suppose I could take Anne with me to the Sunday school picnic this Saturday?

ANNE. Oh, a picnic!

MRS. BARRY. Well, I think that would be for Miss Cuthbert to decide, Diana.

ANNE. Oh, may I, Marilla . . . may I?

DIANA. There's going to be all kinds of races with prizes . . . and we're going to make ice cream.

ANNE. Oh, Marilla, they're going to make ice cream. . . . What's that?

DIANA. . . . Oh, Anne, you're teasing!

MRS. BARRY. I think if the child has never had a taste of it, Marilla, this might be a good opportunity.

MARILLA. Well . . . I suppose if the parents are going along as well . . .

DIANA. Everyone's going!

MARILLA. Well, I don't s'pose there's any harm in it. (ANNE *suddenly embraces* MARILLA.) Land sakes, child, hurry along or you'll be late for school!

(ANNE *and* DIANA *rush off.*)

DIANA. We can go swimming at the picnic too, Anne. Tillie Boulter nearly got drowned last year.

ANNE. Oh, it must be such a romantic experience to have been nearly drowned!

(*They both exit.*)

ACT ONE

SCENE 9

PATCH QUILT AND SCHOOL.

SONG: *"BACK TO SCHOOL"*
(BOYS *and* GIRLS.)

ALL.
THINK OF THE HOMEWORK! GOTTA BE DONE!
THINK OF THE SPELLING BEE . . . THAT'S FUN!
THINK OF THE 'RITHMETIC ON THE SLATE!
THINK ABOUT RECESS . . . CAN'T WAIT!
SCHOOL AGAIN!
SCHOOL AGAIN!
SCHOOL AGAIN!

MOODY. Nix, nix, it's old man Phillips!

(*Everyone freezes.*)

ALL. Good morning, Mr. Phillips! (MR. PHILLIPS *rides through on a bicycle.*)
SCHOOL AGAIN!
SCHOOL AGAIN!
SCHOOL AGAIN!

(TOMMY SLOANE *aims his slingshot off stage. There is is a crash.* MR. PHILLIPS *returns on foot, furious.* TOMMY SLOANE *shakes in his boots.* PRISSY ANDREWS *steps forth and charms* MR. PHILLIPS. *They go off arm in arm.* KIDS *follow.* SCHOOL BALLET: *Skipping rope, tag, leapfrog, hopscotch, and other hi-jinks at the* KIDS *wend their way to school.*)
SCHOOL AGAIN!
SCHOOL AGAIN!
SCHOOL AGAIN!

ACT ONE

SCENE 10

SCHOOL.

Chaos reigns. A cross-eyed likeness of MR. PHILLIPS *has been drawn on the blackboard.*

MR. PHILLIPS *enters with* PRISSY ANDREWS. *Stops. Rubs off board. Restores order by whacking desk with a pointer. He then takes a pitch pipe out of his pocket, motions the* CLASS *to rise.* MR. PHILLIPS *blows pitch pipe.*

SONG: *"AVONLEA, WE LOVE THEE"*

ALL. Hmmmm. (*Out of tune.*)
AVONLEA, WE LOVE THEE.
TO THEE WE PLEDGE, OUR ALMA MATER,
HEADS AND *HANDS* AND *HEARTS* FOREVER,
FOR WE KNOW THAT YOU ARE GRAND.
MR. PHILLIPS. 2-3-4.
ALL.
AVONLEA, ABOVE THEE
WILL RAISE OUR LOYAL SONS AND DAUGHTERS
BANNERS OF SINCERE ENDEAVOR
OVER PRINCE *ED*-WARD *IS*-LAND.

(KIDS *sit down noisily.*)

MR. PHILLIPS. All right, class, now settle down . . . settle down and get on with . . . the work I gave you yesterday. (MR. PHILLIPS *squeezes into the seat beside* PRISSY ANDREWS. ANNE *starts to move out of her seat.*)

DIANA. Don't bother Mr. Phillips now, Anne. He's busy.

ANNE. But he doesn't even know I'm here, Diana.

DIANA. Oh, he doesn't know any of us is here. He spends all his time with that Prissy Andrews. He's getting her ready to try for a scholarship. At least, that's what he *says* he's doing.

ANNE. But what are the rest of us supposed to do?

DIANA. Oh, finish up the work we didn't do yesterday.

ANNE. But I wasn't here yesterday.

DIANA. I know. You lucky thing. Why don't you draw something funny on your slate?

JOSIE. (*Reading a note that has been passed to her.*) Gilbert Blythe, you dirty little . . .

MR. PHILLIPS. All right, class. Settle down and concentrate.

DIANA. That boy teases Josie Pye something terrible. And she's dead gone on him! He's awf'ly handsome, isn't he? His name is Gilbert Blythe.

ANNE. I think he's very bold. (DIANA *giggles.*) When does Mr. Phillips start teaching the rest of us?

DIANA. As soon as he straightens out Prissy Andrews.

GILBERT. Psst! Hey, what are these . . . carrots?

ANNE. You mean, hateful boy! How dare you! (ANNE *breaks her slate over* GILBERT BLYTHE'S *head.*)

MR. PHILLIPS. (*Rising.*) Who is this strange girl?

ANNE. Anne Shirley, sir. I'm new. . . . I have a note.

MR. PHILLIPS. And what does all this mean?

GILBERT. It was my fault, sir. I teased her.

MR. PHILLIPS. Sit down, Blythe. I am sorry to see a new pupil displaying such a vindictive spirit. What did you say your name was?

ANNE. Anne Shirley, sir. Anne with an "e" . . .

MR. PHILLIPS. Class repeat after me . . . "Anne Shirley has a very bad temper."

(JOSIE PYE *writes this on the blackboard, omitting the "e" in* ANNE.)

CLASS. Anne Shirley has a very bad temper.

MR. PHILLIPS. Anne Shirley must control her temper.

ANNE. Oh, please, sir! She's spelled it wrong! She forgot the "e."

MR. PHILLIPS. You must learn to control your tongue as well as your temper. Go and sit with Gilbert Blythe. . . . Did you hear what I said?

ANNE. Yes. But I didn't suppose you really meant it.

MR. PHILLIPS. I assure you that I did. Obey me at once. . . .

Class repeat after me . . . "Anne Shirley has a very bad temper."

CLASS. Anne Shirley has a very bad temper.

MR. PHILLIPS. Anne Shirley must control her temper.

CLASS. Anne Shirley must control her temper.

MOODY. . . . trol her temper.

MR. PHILLIPS. Moody Spurgeon MacPherson. Come here. Here. Here! (*Hits himself on the hand with the pointer, which breaks in two. Laughter from* CLASS.)

MOODY. (*After* CLASS.) Ahh-ha-ha . . . (*Gulp.*)

MR. PHILLIPS. What have you got in your mouth? Have you been chewing pine gum again?

MOODY. No, sir, I was just soaking a prune for recess.

MR. PHILLIPS. Well, get rid of it! (*He does. In* MR. PHILLIPS' *outstretched hand.* CLASS *laughs again.*) All right, recess! Except for Blythe and the new girl. Gilbert, you stay in and clean off the board. The rest of you, dismiss in an orderly fashion . . .

(CLASS *exits like a stampede of buffaloes.* GILBERT *and* ANNE *are left alone in the classroom.*)

SONG: *"WONDRIN' "*

GILBERT.
WONDRIN'.
ALL AT ONCE I'M WONDRIN'
WHAT IT'S LIKE TO GROW UP
AND HAVE SOMEONE SHOW UP
WHO'LL BE
AWFUL NICE AND YOU'LL BE
SUCH A SILLY FOOL SHE'LL
NEVER LOOK YOUR WAY.

WONDRIN'.
NOW THEY'LL ALL BE WONDRIN'
AND THEY'LL GAB LIKE PARROTS
'CAUSE I CALLED HER "CARROTS" . . .
WONDRIN'
WHAT IT WAS THAT HIT ME
AND BLUNDRIN'
LIKE I MIGHT BE WONDRIN'
IF SHE MIGHT BE WONDRIN'
ABOUT ME THIS WAY.
    (*Spoken.*)
Anne, I'm sorry your slate got broken—I— (ANNE *suddenly rushes out.*)

WONDRIN'
WHAT IT WAS THAT HIT ME
AND BLUNDRIN'
LIKE I MIGHT BE WONDRIN'
IF SHE MIGHT BE WONDRIN'
ABOUT ME . . . THIS . . . WAY.

ACT ONE

SCENE 11

PATCH WORK DROP.

MRS. PYE *alone on stage is joined by an excited* JOSIE.

SONG: *"DID YOU HEAR?"*
(JOSIE, MRS. PYE, OTHERS.)

JOSIE.
DID YOU HEAR? DID YOU HEAR?
    MRS. PYE.
TELL ME EVERYTHING, MY DEAR,
AND I PROMISE YOU I'LL NEVER TELL A SOUL!
    (JOSIE *whispers eight bars and gestures the violence of the
    slate incident.* MRS. PYE *is aghast at what she hears.*)
WHY, THERE OUGHT TO BE A LAW!
    JOSIE.
THAT'S EXACTLY WHAT I SAW!
    MRS. PYE.
SHE TOOK THE SLATE, AND SUDDENLY WENT
    BERSERK?
    JOSIE.
CROSS MY HEART, HOPE TO DIE:
HAVE I EVER TOLD A LIE?
    MRS. PYE.
SHE'S A TERROR, SHE'S A TARTAR, SHE'S A TURK!
DID YOU HEAR? DID YOU HEAR?
    MRS. BARRY.
TELL ME EVERYTHING, MY DEAR . . .
AND I PROMISE YOU I'LL NEVER TELL A SOUL!
    (MRS. PYE *whispers eight bars.* MRS. BARRY'S *eyes widen.*)
I WOULD THRASH HER WHEN SHE'S CAUGHT!
    MRS. PYE.
THAT'S EXACTLY WHAT I THOUGHT!

Mrs. Barry.
BUT YOU SAY THE DOCTOR HAD TO TAKE A
    STITCH?
Josie.
THREE OR FOUR, MAYBE MORE,
Mrs. Pye.
I WAS WATCHING FROM THE DOOR.
Mrs. Barry.
SHE'S A MONSTER, SHE'S A FURY, SHE'S A WITCH!
(*Exits.*)
Josie. (*Loud aside to audience.*)
SHE HAS SET HER CAP FOR GILBERT BLYTHE.
IT'S AS PLAIN AS PLAIN CAN BE.
IF SHE WANTS HIM SHE WILL HAVE TO DEAL
    WITH ME.
Mrs. Barry. (*Enters, leans on counter of store.*)
DID YOU HEAR? DID YOU HEAR?
Lucilla. (*The store clerk.*)
TELL ME EVERYTHING, MY DEAR,
YOU CAN TRUST ME AND YOU KNOW MY LIPS
    ARE SEALED.
DID YOU HEAR? DID YOU HEAR?
Farmer and Mailman.
TELL US EVERYTHING, MY DEAR,
AND WE PROMISE IT WILL NEVER BE REVEALED.
Lucilla.
THEY SHOULD PUT THE GIRL AWAY.
Mrs. Barry.
THAT'S EXACTLY WHAT I SAY.
Mailman.
YOU MEAN SHE WENT AND SPLIT HIS SKULL IN
    TWO?
Josie.
I WAS THERE, AND I SWEAR
THERE WAS BLOOD JUST EVERYWHERE.
Mrs. Barry.
SHE'S A VIXEN.
Mrs. Pye.
SHE'S A HUSSY.
Mrs. Lynde. (*Entering.*)
WHO?

    (*All the* Women *whisper in* Mrs. Lynde's *ear.*)

Josie.
WE DON'T WANT HER KIND IN AVONLEA

AND I HOPE SHE LEAVES TONIGHT.
IF THEY EXPEL HER THEN I'LL TELL HER,
"SERVES YOU RIGHT!"
    MARILLA. Hello, Josie; afternoon, Rachel, ladies.
    MRS. LYNDE. Now, Marilla, heaven knows I'm no gossip, but
I'm sure you'd want to be the first to know.
DID YOU HEAR? DID YOU HEAR?
    MARILLA.
I WILL, NEVER FEAR. YOU ALWAYS HAVE A LITTLE
    BIT OF NEWS.
    ALL.
WELL I NEVER, DID YOU EVER,
I SUPPOSE SHE THINKS SHE'S CLEVER,
HE'LL BE MARKED FOR LIFE,
WITH SUCH AN AWFUL BRUISE.
    MARILLA.
IN THE SCHOOLROOM SPLIT HIS HEAD?
    JOSIE.
I THINK GILBERT'S GOOD AS DEAD.
    MARILLA.
HE WAS TOOK BY MOTORCAR TO
    CHARLOTTETOWN?
    ALL.
SHE'S A PIECE OF SATAN'S FINEST HANDIWORK!
SHE'S A VIXEN.
    MRS. PYE.
SHE'S A HUSSY!
    LUCILLA.
SHE'S A TERROR!
    MRS. BARRY.
SHE'S A TARTAR!
    JOSIE.
WE DON'T WANT HER KIND IN AVONLEA!
    ALL.
TERRIBLE TEMPERED TURK!

BLACKOUT

ACT ONE

SCENE 12

FLOWER SCRIM.

ANNE *and* DIANA *are walking home from school.*

DIANA. Cheer up, Anne. You mustn't mind Gilbert making fun of your hair. He's called me a crow a dozen times.

ANNE. There's a great deal of difference between a crow and a carrot, Diana. Gilbert Blythe has hurt my feelings excruciatingly. (DIANA *giggles.*) Isn't that a scrumptious word? It took me weeks to learn how to say it right.

MATTHEW. (*Entering.*) Well now, what did you learn your first day at school?

ANNE. Oh, Matthew . . . Diana invited me to her Sunday school picnic. I've never been to a picnic.

MATTHEW. Well, you know, neither have I. Marilla doesn't think the Good Lord intended us to eat outdoors.

ANNE. Don't you think a picnic is the very nicest way to enter the church?

MARILLA. (*Entering quickly with* MRS. BARRY.) There'll be no picnic for you, young lady!

MRS. BARRY. Come along home, Diana!

DIANA. But, Mother . . .

MRS. BARRY. (*Exits dragging* DIANA.) Home! At once!

MARILLA. There'll be no picnics or anything else 'til you stop disgracing our name with your vicious temper!

MATTHEW. Oh, now, Marilla. It can't be as bad as all that.

MARILLA. This child is uncontrollable. She's given the Blythe boy a concussion and right at this moment he's in the Charlottetown hospital with four doctors pickin' the slate out of his head!

ANNE. That's not true! That's just not true!

MARILLA. Don't you contradict me, young lady! I got it from Rachel Lynde and she got it from the girl who works at the yards good counter at the store and she was there and saw the whole thing. Why, the boy's brain pan was split wide open for all to see.

(GILBERT *runs in.*)

GILBERT. Anne . . . Anne. I'm sorry I broke you. ate, and I brought you a new one.

MARILLA. Why, Gilbert Blythe! What are you doing up and around?

GILBERT. Excuse me, Miss Cuthbert, but I came over to make amends to Anne for what I did.

MARILLA. For what you did? I thought it was her that had done it to you!

MATTHEW. Whatever it was.

GILBERT. Oh, it was nothing really. I teased her in school and she got the blame. But it was all my fault.

MATTHEW. Oh . . . how's your brain pan?

GILBERT. My what, sir?

MATTHEW. The part of you that's split wide open with four doctors pickin' at you. . . .

GILBERT. I think somebody has been giving you a story, Mr. Cuthbert.

MATTHEW. Uh-huh.

MARILLA. I should have known better than to listen to those gossips that hang around Blair's store.

MATTHEW. And we must be certain Mrs. Barry gets the story straight, too . . . now I don't see any reason why Anne shouldn't go to that Sunday school picnic.

ANNE. Oh, could I?

GILBERT. Would it be all right if she went with me? I'd promise to look after her and bring her home on time.

MATTHEW. Well, now, I think that would be just . . .

MARILLA. Well, I'd want somebody to be responsible for her.

ANNE. No!! If I go at all I shall accompany Miss Diana Barry! I and she can look after each other!

MARILLA. Anne!

ANNE. The iron has entered my soul. (*Exits.*)

(*MUSIC.* CHILDREN *and* ADULTS *on their way to the picnic.* FARMER *and* MAILMAN *share a quick drink. The* MINISTER *goes past, seizes the flask.* SEVERAL LADIES *pass, he waves to them, forgetting he has a flask in his hand, and a new rumor starts in Avonlea.* MR. PHILLIPS *escorts* PRISSY ANDREWS, *and picks pieces of straw from her back.* JOSIE PYE *drags* GILBERT BLYTHE. *She hopes to snare him with a basket of sandwiches.*)

ACT ONE

SCENE 13

PATCH QUILT AND PICNIC.

GILBERT. I'm hungry now.
JOSIE. I made a lot of sandwiches . . . deviled egg with choke-cherry jelly.
GILBERT. I'm not *that* hungry.

(ANNE *enters with* DIANA.)

ANNE. I can't wait 'til we get at the ice cream.
DIANA. Oh, Anne, you'll love it!

SONG: *"ICE CREAM"*

ICE CREAM!
IS ANYTHING MORE DELECTABLE
THAN ICE CREAM?
WHY, EVEN THE MOST RESPECTABLE
EAT ICE CREAM.
IT'S WONDERFUL ON A SUMMER'S AFTERNOON
IN JUNE.
ICE CREAM,
THE RECIPE'S SOMETHING SERIOUS
BUT ICE CREAM
MAKES EVERYONE SO DELIRIOUS
THAT ICE CREAM
IS CERTAINLY WORTH THE TROUBLE THAT
    IT TAKES . . .
    ANNE. What does it take?
    DIANA.
IT TAKES A TIN PAIL, PACK IT WITH SOME ICE,
ROCK SALT, SPRINKLE IT ON TWICE,
BIG SPOON TO SEE IF IT TASTES NICE!
    ANNE. You've got me aquiver, I'm starting to shiver!
FOR . . .
    CHORUS.
ICE CREAM,
THE MIXING IS MOST ENJOYABLE
OF ICE CREAM
AND NO ONE IS UNEMPLOYABLE
IN OUR SCHEME.

YOU'VE GOT TO KEEP ON THE DOUBLE TILL IT'S
    SET,
YOU BET!
    LADIES.
CHILL MIX. COVER IT UP TIGHT!
TURN CRANK.
    JOSIE.
CAN'T YOU DO IT RIGHT?
    DIANA.
YOU HELP!!
    ALL.
THIS IS NO TIME TO FIGHT!

KEEP ON WITH THE TURNING
AND SOON WE'LL BE CHURNING OUT

ICE CREAM
IS OUT OF THIS WORLD FOR TASTINESS
BUT ICE CREAM
CAN NEVER BE MADE WITH HASTINESS
SO OUR DREAM
IS BOUND TO BE JUST A LITTLE OVERDUE!
HOW TRUE!!

MINISTER. Everybody ready for the three-legged race! (*Everyone pairs off and ties their legs together.* MR. PHILLIPS, *in his
excitement, ties his leg not to* PRISSY ANDREWS, *but to the*
MINISTER.) Mr. Phillips!!! (*To her horror,* ANNE SHIRLEY *finds
that she is yoked to* GILBERT BLYTHE.) THREE-LEGGED
RACE. The winners, Anne Shirley, spelled with an "e," and
Gilbert Blythe. Everybody ready for the egg and spoon race.
(EGG AND SPOON RACE. *The* CHILDREN *race off with spoons
in their mouths with an egg balanced precariously on the other
end. A keen eye can observe* GILBERT BLYTHE *holding back* JOISE
PYE, *contriving to let* ANNE *win.* ANNE *is first to hit the finish
line.*) The winner Anne Shirley!

ANNE. Oh, Diana, what a thrill. I never thought I'd win!

DIANA. Yes, and Gilbert held them back, so you'd be the first
one in!

ANNE. Humiliating!

DIANA. I think he wants to be your beau.

ANNE. No! I shall hate Gilbert Blythe for the rest of my
life. . . .

JOSIE. That's good. 'Cause *he's mine.*

DIANA. He is not!

JOSIE. He is too!

MRS. BARRY. It's ready!!

ALL.

NOW . . . IT'S FROZEN TO THE CORE,
'BOUT TIME, MY ARM WAS GETTING SORE.
HERE'S THE MOMENT WE'VE BEEN WAITING
    FOR . . .

GILBERT. There you are, Miss Shirley, your first taste of ice
cr . . .

(JOSIE *trips* GILBERT *and the ice cream cone lands square in*
    ANNE'S *face.*)

ANNE. Gilbert Blythe! I'll . . . I'll . . . I . . . I . . .
(*Suddenly her taste buds are aware of a new sensation.*)
ICE . . . CREAM . . .
IT'S MARVELOUS AND MYSTERIOUS,
ICE CREAM.

(GILBERT, *embarrassed, stomps off, leaving* ANNE *torn between
    following* GILBERT *and the new-found delight of ice cream.*)

ALL.
ICE . . . CREAM . . .
IT'S WONDERFUL ON A SUMMER'S AFTERNOON
IN JUNE.
ICE CREAM!
ICE CREAM!!

CURTAIN

END OF ACT ONE

ACT TWO

Scene 1

OUTSIDE THE FENCE AT AVONLEA SCHOOL.

GILBERT BLYTHE *sits barefoot, savoring the last moments of freedom.*

SONG: *"SUMMER"*

GILBERT.
WHY AIN'T IT ALWAYS SUMMER?
I COULD SLEEP LATE,
AND STAY UP TILL MIDNIGHT CATCHIN'
DEW WORMS FOR BAIT.
NOW I'LL BE COMBED AND CURRIED
AND WORRIED AGAIN.
WHO WANTS TO PUT THEIR SHOES ON?
NOT ME, MY FRIEND!
    JOSIE. (*Entering.*)
I GREW A WHOLE INCH BIGGER!
    GERRY. (*Entering.*)
I LOST A WISDOM TOOTH!
    ANNE. (*Popping up behind the fence.*)
I TOOK A BIG UMBRELLA
AND FELL OFF OUR ROOF!
    DIANA. (*Also from behind the fence.*)
I HAD A TASTE OF HIGH LIFE
IN CHARLOTTETOWN!
THEY HAVE ELECTRIC LIGHTS THERE
THAT NEVER BURN DOWN!
I SAW THE LIGHTS ON QUEEN STREET,
A KEEN STREET FOR CLOTHES.
AND I HAD A CHERRY PROSPHATE
WENT UP MY NOSE!

(OTHER KIDS *arrive.*)

TILLIE, TOMMY and GERTIE.
WE FOUND A GORGEOUS SEASHELL!

44

Ruby and Moody.
WE FOUND SOME LICORICE ROOT!
    Charlie.
I FOUND THE HIRED GIRL SWIMMIN'
IN HER BIRTHDAY SUIT!
    All.
WHERE DID THE SUMMER GO TO?
WE HAD SUCH FUN!
NOW WE GO BACK TO CAESAR
AND ATTILA THE HUN.
I'M SURE THAT ALL THIS LATIN
WILL FLATTEN MY HEAD:
SIC TRANSIT GLORIA MUNDI.
SUMMERTIME'S DEAD . . . SUMMERTIME'S . . .
    SUMMERTIME'S . . .

WHO WANTS TO PUT THEIR SHOES ON?
NOT ME, MY FRIEND!

(SHOE DANCE. *The* Boys *put their boots on and dance. They find them extremely uncomfortable. Finally they can stand it no longer and exit happily barefoot.* Anne *and* Diana *wander on, followed briskly by* Josie Pye.)

Josie. Last year I concentrated on geography and it didn't get me anywhere. This year I'm going to concentrate on boys. I intend to have half a dozen beaux all crazy about me.
    Anne. Wouldn't you just as soon have one in his right mind?
    Diana. You already have that, Anne. I hear that Gilbert Blythe has a terrible crush on you.
    Josie. Who said? I heard Gilbert tell Charlie Sloane just the other day that when Anne Shirley sings in church her Adam's apple bobs in and out like a chicken pecking dirt!
    Gilbert. (*Entering.*) Excuse me, girls. I'd like to talk to Anne. Alone! (*Takes* Anne *aside.*) Look, Anne . . . can't we start off this year by being friends? I'm sorry I made fun of your hair that time. I only meant it for a joke.

(Anne *wants to make up, but at that moment she sees* Josie *sticking her neck out "like a chicken pecking dirt."*)

    Anne. No! Gilbert Blythe. . . . Never!
    Gilbert. All right! I don't care either! Carrots!! Come on, Josie! (*Stalks off, deliberately putting his arm around* Josie.)
    Anne. Oh, Diana, let's promise each other one thing. That

when we grow up, neither of us will get married but live together forever as nice old maids.

DIANA. Oh, I don't know if I want to be an old maid forever, Anne. I always thought the nicest thing would be to marry a wicked young man and gradually reform him.

ANNE. I know. . . . I know, when we grow up you're going to get married and leave me! Oh, I hate your husband!

DIANA. Ohhhh, Anne . . . that's hundreds of years away! Besides, you know I'll always, always be your best and closest friend.

ANNE. Diana, I shall hold you to that till death do us apart.

SONG: *"KINDRED SPIRITS"*

ANNE.
KINDRED SPIRITS
JUST YOU AND ME, EVER TO BE
BOTH.
KINDRED SPIRITS
ANNE.
SHARING OUR JOYS,
DIANA.
EVEN THE BOYS!
ANNE.
WE MUST SOLEMNLY SWEAR,
DIANA.
SWEARING'S A *SIN!*
(*She giggles.*)
SHALL WE BEGIN?
BOTH.
NOW WE'RE KINDRED SPIRITS
ANNE.
LOYAL AND TRUE,
DIANA.
TRUER THAN BLUE.
BOTH.
ALL OUR LIFE THROUGH, WE TWO.

LIKE A FLY STICKS TO GLUE
DIANA.
WE'LL STICK TOGETHER
ANNE.
JUST ME AND YOU
DIANA.
JUST YOU AND ME

ANNE.
JUST YOU AND *I*
   DIANA.
THAT'S HOW IT MUST BE,
NOW WE'RE KINDRED SPIRITS
FAITHFUL AND TRUE
   ANNE.
LIKE AN OLD SHOE
   BOTH.
ALL OUR LIFE THROUGH, WE TWO.

(*The board fence disappears and they are with the rest of the* PUPILS *in the schoolyard.*)

ACT TWO

SCENE 2

SCHOOLYARD.

The new teacher, MURIEL STACY, *enters.*

MISS STACY. Good morning, boys and girls.

CHARLIE. Hey! You're not Mr. Phillips.

MISS STACY. No, I'm not. My name is Muriel Stacy, and I'm your new teacher. Mr. Phillips won't be coming back.

ALL. Hurray!

CHARLIE. Why not?

MISS STACY. Well, I believe he has another job . . . a better paying one . . . at the feed store.

GILBERT. (*Snickering to* TOMMY SLOANE.) I heard he had to marry Prissy Andrews!

MISS STACY. My, what a bright sunny morning! I think we'll have our first class right out here in the yard.

DIANA. Outside!

MISS STACY. Why not? Just because a pupil is slumped over a desk writing something in a copybook it doesn't necessarily mean he's learning anything. Yes, we'll have our first class outside!

ANNE. Diana, Miss Stacy's a kindred spirit.

SONG: *"OPEN THE WINDOW"*

MISS STACY.
OPEN THE WINDOW. SWEEP OUT THE COBWEBS.

OPEN YOUR MIND TO WHAT IS GOING ON ALL
    AROUND.
LOOK AT THE SUNLIGHT. WHAT IS IT MADE OF?
HOW CAN IT MAKE THE FLOWERS JUMP RIGHT
    OUT OF THE GROUND?

OPEN YOUR EARS. USE THAT OLD NOSE.
HOW COME A QUEEN BEE . . . KNOWS A ROSE?
TAKE OFF THE BLINKERS. LET IN THE DAYLIGHT.
WHY DOES THE CLINGING IVY CLING?
TEAR DOWN THE FENCES. USE THOSE FIVE
    SENSES.
LEARN EVERYTHING!
Now, are there any questions?

TILLIE. Miss Stacy, what *is* the sunlight made of?

MISS STACY. It's made of energy! And it's coming to you at
the rate of 186,000 miles a second!

MOODY. Gee whillikers! I never knew that!

MISS STACY.

OPEN YOUR HANDS! REACH FOR THE SKIES!

GILBERT. . . . How does a lobster . . .

MISS STACY. Yes?

GILBERT. Fertilize?

(*Some of the* BOYS *laugh.*)

MISS STACY.

LOOK ALL AROUND YOU! LIFE WILL ASTOUND
    YOU!
WHAT MAKES THE YELLOW WARBLER SING?
OPEN YOUR HEART, TOO! NOW WE WILL START TO
LEARN EVERYTHING.
Now our first class today will be . . .

CHARLIE. LAAAtin . . .

ALL. Yeh!

MISS STACY. No, not yet . . .

JOSIE. Algebra?

MISS STACY. Later.

GERRY. De-PORT-ment?

MISS STACY. That comes naturally with a healthy mind, in a
healthy body.

ANNE. Then what, Miss Stacy?

MISS STACY. Nature study!

OPEN THE WINDOW!

ALL.

OPEN THE WINDOW!

Miss Stacy.
SWEEP OUT THE COBWEBS!
All.
SWEEP OUT THE COBWEBS!
Miss Stacy.
OPEN YOUR MIND TO WHAT IS GOING ON
  AROUND.
LOOK AT THE SUNLIGHT!
All.
LOOK AT THE SUNLIGHT!
Miss Stacy.
WHAT IS IT MADE OF?
All.
WHAT IS IT MADE OF?
Miss Stacy.
HOW CAN IT MAKE THE FLOWERS JUMP RIGHT
  OUT
OF THE GROUND? TAKE OFF THE BLINKERS!
All.
TAKE OFF THE BLINKERS!
Miss Stacy.
LET IN THE DAYLIGHT!
All.
LET IN THE DAYLIGHT!
Miss Stacy.
TEAR DOWN THE FENCES!
All.
TEAR DOWN THE FENCES!
Miss Stacy.
USE YOUR FIVE SENSES!
All.
USE YOUR FIVE SENSES!
LEARN EVERYTHING.
Miss Stacy.
OPEN THE WINDOW. ROLL UP THE BLIND THERE.
AND YOU WILL FIND THERE IS A PARADISE
  ALL ABLAZE.
LISTEN TO MUSIC. LOOK AT A STATUE.
BEAUTY COMES AT YOU IN A THOUSAND
  DIFFERENT WAYS.
DREAM UP A DREAM. MAKE IT COME TRUE.
MAN MADE AN AEROPLANE . . . AND IT FLEW.
OPEN THE TAP NOW. TAKE OFF THE CAP NOW.
LET YOUR IMAGINATION SWING.
TEAR DOWN THE FENCES, USE ALL YOUR SENSES,

ALL.
LEARN EVERYTHING!

(*DROP CURTAIN.* ANNE *and* DIANA *walking home from school.*)

SONG: *"KINDRED SPIRITS"* (Reprise)

DIANA and ANNE.
KINDRED SPIRITS . . .
ANNE.
HAVING ONE AIM
DIANA.
THINKING THE SAME.
BOTH.
KINDRED SPIRITS
DIANA.
MISS STACY AND WE.
ANNE.
NOW WE ARE THREE.
     (DIANA *leaves* ANNE.)
FINDING ONE BOSOM FRIEND
MAY LEAD TO OTHER
FRIENDS IN THE END.

(ANNE *sees* MATTHEW *waiting for her at the gate.*)

ACT TWO

SCENE 3

GREEN GABLES.

MATTHEW. Anne of Green Gables . . . (*Hands her some wild flowers.*)
ANNE. Oh, Matthew!
MATTHEW. Well now, what did you learn on your first day back at school?
ANNE. (*Going into the house.*) The first thing I learned is that we have a new teacher and she's absolutely perfect!

(MARILLA *is sweeping the floor.*)

MATTHEW. Well, that is good news!

ANNE. And when she pronounces my name I feel instinctively that she's spelling it with an "e." Matthew, her sleeve puffs are bigger than anybody else's in Avonlea. Honestly, Marilla, she has to come through the door sideways.

MARILLA. I hope you managed to notice what she was teaching.

ANNE. (*Putting flowers in a vase.*) We took a walk through Sloane's woods. It's called a field trip, and afterwards we had to deliver out loud, an oral composition about "What I Saw On Our Field Trip" and I gave the best one.

MATTHEW. Well now, what did I tell you . . .

MARILLA. It's very vain of you to say so, Anne. You'd best let your teacher say it.

ANNE. Oh, but she *did* say it.

MATTHEW. Who came second?

ANNE. Oh . . . Gil . . . one of the boys. I forget his name. But the best thing of all is going to be every other Friday. That's when we'll have recitations, and after Christmas we're going to put on a concert. (*Gets the dustpan to help* MARILLA.)

MATTHEW. Well!

MARILLA. Fiddlesticks! More foolishness!

ANNE. Oh, no. Miss Stacy says this shall be a feast of reason and a flow of soul. (*Makes a sweeping gesture and the contents of the dustpan are scattered all over.*)

MARILLA. Oh, does she? Well, I don't believe in concerts. They spoil young people for everyday life. Just a chance for boys and girls to stay up late and carry on when they'd be *better* off in bed. (*Exits with dustpan.*)

MATTHEW. Is Gilbert Blythe going to be with you in the concert? I saw him last Sunday in church. He was standing there looking tall and manly just like his father. You know, John Blythe and Marilla used to be good friends. In fact, some folks said John was Marilla's beau.

ANNE. Oh, Matthew, what happened?

MATTHEW. They had a quarrel. And Marilla wouldn't forgive him when he asked her to. I guess she . . . meant to—but, well, you know how Marilla is. . . .

(MARILLA *comes back into the kitchen.*)

MARILLA. Now don't go away, Anne. I'll need you upstairs in a moment. (*Aside to* MATTHEW.) And not a word out of you, mind. (*Goes upstairs.*)

ANNE. I could almost imagine Marilla is being mysterious.

MATTHEW. She has a surprise for you.

ANNE. Oh, Matthew! What is it?

MATTHEW. Well now, I'm not supposed to say.

ANNE. A new dress! Marilla has made me a new dress. Oh, I just know it! Oh, I can't wait to see it. Oh, Matthew, is it a new dress, is it?

MARILLA. (*From the bedroom.*) Anne, upstairs!

MATTHEW. Now remember, *I* never told you.

(ANNE *is removing her old dress as she runs up the stairs.*)

MARILLA. (*Presenting the new dress.*) I had some material left over so I made you a nice sash. Well, how do you like it?

ANNE. I *imagine* that I like it.

MARILLA. I don't want you to imagine it. What's wrong with it? It's new, isn't it?

ANNE. Yes. . . .

MARILLA. Then why don't you like it? It's sensible and it's serviceable. I should think you'd be grateful.

ANNE. Oh, but I *am* grateful. Of course, I'd be ever so much gratefuller if you'd made it with puffed sleeves.

MARILLA. Fiddlesticks!

ANNE. Everybody else at school has them.

MARILLA. Those ridiculous-looking things.

MATTHEW. (*Who has trudged all the way upstairs.*) Now, Marilla, look here!

MARILLA. Look where?

MATTHEW. Marilla, why don't we . . .

MARILLA. Why don't we what?

MATTHEW. Well, why shouldn't she . . .

MARILLA. Exactly! Why shouldn't she? I prefer these plain sensible things.

ANNE. But wouldn't you rather look ridiculous when everybody else does than plain and sensible all by yourself?

MARILLA. It's wicked to think of your looks so much.

MATTHEW. Marilla, I think if we could . . . if she should . . . oh, you can't just take a girl and . . .

MARILLA. Matthew Cuthbert, I don't know what you're trying to say but whatever it is, keep it to yourself. This is women's affairs; now you stay out of it! (MATTHEW *goes downstairs.* MARILLA *follows.*) I'm afraid you're a very vain little girl.

ANNE. How can I be vain when I *know* I'm homely?

MARILLA. She doesn't like it. Good green wincey, and she doesn't like it. (*Goes out screen door.*)

ANNE. . . . Just like a chicken pecking dirt. The world has laughed long enough. Now is the time to take my fate in my own hands. (ANNE *opens a drawer and dramatically holds a dark green bottle aloft.*) It is a far, far better thing I do . . . I am standing on the threshold of eternity at last, as reckless of the future as I have been of the past!

(*Bedroom drop comes down.* MATTHEW *is alone in the kitchen.*)

SONG: *"THE WORDS"*

MATTHEW.
THE WORDS! THE WORDS! THE WORDS!
WHY WON'T THEY COME WHEN I WANT THEM?
I'VE KEPT MY PEACE SINCE I WAS YOUNG
FOR A BOY IS TAUGHT TO HOLD HIS TONGUE:
BUT NOW WHEN I'M BUSTIN' TO SAY MY SAY
I JUST CAN'T SEEM TO FIND THE WAY. . . .

I CAN'T FIND THE WORDS . . .
CAN'T GET OUT THE PHRASES.
JUST WHEN SHE NEEDS LOVE
I CAN'T SING HER PRAISES.
WHERE DO THE WORDS GO
WHEN I AM BEFORE HER?
OH, IF I COULD SHOW
WHAT I FEEL IN MY HEART,
I'D IMPLORE HER.
I ADORE HER.
I'D DIE FOR HER:
BUT I CAN'T FIND THE WORDS.

(MATTHEW *leaves the kitchen in utter frustration.*)

ACT TWO

SCENE 4

GREEN GABLES.

MARILLA. (*Coming into the kitchen.*) Whooohooo . . . ! Anne, you may use some of this cream for Diana's berries. . . . Where is that child? Up in her room practisin' for that Tom Fool concert, (*Goes upstairs.*) I suppose. She has no business daydreaming when we're expecting company. Anne? Humph. Not here. Diana and Mizz Barry'll be here in less than 5 minutes and her bed not made, mercy on us! (*Something has moved in the bed.*) What are you doing here? Have you been asleep?

ANNE. No.

MARILLA. You're not sick?

ANNE. No—but please, Marilla, just go away and don't look at me.

MARILLA. What nonsense! Get up! The both of us are expectin' company for tea in less than 5 minutes!!

ANNE. Please go away and don't look at me!

MARILLA. Did anyone ever hear the like? Anne Shirley, get right up this minute and— (*Snatches off the covers and gets the shock of her life.*) ahh!!!! . . . your hair? It's *green!!*

ANNE. I thought nothing could be worse than red hair . . . so I dyed it.

MARILLA. But it's positively green!

ANNE. Now I know it's ten times worse to have green hair.

MARILLA. Whatever made you do such a wicked thing?

ANNE. He told me it would make my hair a beautiful raven black . . . he positively assured me it would.

MARILLA. He told you? Who told you? What are you talking about?

ANNE. You remember the pedlar that was here last month . . . I bought it from him.

MARILLA. That foreigner! I sent him away, I only deal with the Watkins man.

ANNE. I know, but after I bought it I put it away, because I didn't have the nerve to try it . . . until you . . .

MARILLA. Until I made you a dress . . .

ANNE. Oh, Marilla, it wasn't that. Not just that. It was Josie Pye . . . oh, just everything!

MARILLA. There, there, child. This is a fast dye if ever there was one. It's a good job you didn't use it on the top of your head first.

ANNE. Oh, Marilla, my career is closed!

MARILLA. Now, now, Anne, there's no use crying over spilt . . . whatever it was. That hair will have to come off. I'll get the scissors.

ANNE. But, Marilla . . .

MARILLA. (*Thrusting the scissors into* ANNE'S *hands.*) No time to lose. Here come the ladies up the drive now. (*BEDROOM DROP DESCENDS.* MARILLA *goes downstairs to meet the* LADIES.) Afternoon, Rachel, Valeda, Minnie . . .

RACHEL. Ohhh, are we havin' the meetin' in the kitchen?

MARILLA. Law, no, Mrs. Barry's little girl, Diana, is coming over to have tea with our Anne, that's all.

MRS. SPENCER. How sweet. Just like the big folks.

MRS. PYE. They soon will be big folks. My Josie's growing so fast, just like pigweed in the night.

MRS. LYNDE. I saw the pair of them, Anne and Diana, coming home from school the other day. Growin' like sixty! Now I've always thought that Barry girl was a beauty, and so she is, but I want to tell you, Marilla, I was wrong about your Anne, and I'll admit it in front of the ladies of the Executive. It's not often that I'll admit that I was wrong, but I was, and I'm glad of it. Why, it's little short of wonderful the improvement in your Anne. (ANNE *comes downstairs, her newly-shorn hair covered by a wide sash.*) Really good-lookin' she's getting to be. Why, here she is! How *are* you, Anne?

ANNE. I'm well in body although considerably rumpled in spirit, thank you, ma'am.

MRS. LYNDE. Oh, isn't she polite? Isn't that a new dress we're wearing? What color is it?

MARILLA. It's . . . bottle green.

MRS. LYNDE. I don't think it suits the child.

MRS. PYE. Sallows her some.

MARILLA. Why don't we have the meeting outside, it's such a nice day. Mizz Barry'll be along any minute: That'll make a full turnout. (LADIES *go outside.*) I'll see to the ladies, Anne, you look after Diana. You may open that little yellow crock of cherry preserves if you wish. It's time it was used up anyhow . . . I think it's beginning to work. And if you want you may finish up the raspberry cordial . . . you look just fine . . . considerin'. And that sash does a good job of hiding your hair. The cordial's on the second shelf. (MRS. BARRY *and* DIANA *appear at kitchen door.*) Afternoon, Mrs. Barry, Diana. It's such a nice day we thought we'd have the meeting outside. (*Exits.*)

MRS. BARRY. I'll join you in a minute. Come along, Diana. (MRS. BARRY *and* DIANA *step inside the kitchen.*)

ANNE. The second shelf. . . . Oh! Good afternoon, Mrs. Barry, Diana.

MRS. BARRY. Thank you, Anne. Diana, what do you say?

DIANA. Anne! Your hair! You've put it up! It looks just like the pompadour on the mannequin in Holman's window in Charlottetown. Oh, Mother, when can I put my hair up like that?

MRS. BARRY. Not for another two years, dear, you know that.

DIANA. Well, can I get a sash for my hair like Anne has?

MRS. BARRY. We'll see, dear.

MARILLA. (*Off.*) Mrs. Barry, we're about ready to begin the meetin' now!

MRS. BARRY. Now behave yourself, Diana. (*Exits.*)

MRS. LYNDE. (*Off.*) We will now have the minutes of the last meeting read by Mizz Minnie Pye. . . .

(*Scattered applause is heard.*)

DIANA. Oh, Anne, you are the luckiest thing. I envy you, I really do. I'm absolutely *green!*

ANNE. Won't you please sit down, Diana? Won't you please have some raspberry cordial?

DIANA. This is going to be fun. We can pretend we're grown up and say things to each other we really don't mean. Do you suppose Rachel Lynde and Marilla did this when they were little girls?

ANNE. I don't think I can imagine Mrs. Lynde or Marilla as a little girl. Even my imagination has its limits.

DIANA. May I have some more cordial please?

ANNE. There you are. I'll get the cake. I baked it myself so I hope it's all right. Last time was when the minister came and instead of vanilla I used Sloan's liniment by mistake. . . . Have some more cordial, won't you, Diana.

DIANA. (*Has already helped herself and continues to do so.*) Thank you.

ANNE. You're welcome. Oh, dear, I put too much starch in these napkins. I made a plate of taffy too, but Marilla made me throw it out. One of the cats from the barn walked all over it. I don't think you would have noticed, except for the rather interesting design.

DIANA. (*Giggles.*)
KINDRED SPIRITS JUST YOU AND ME
EVER TO BE . . .

ANNE. I'm so glad you feel that way, Diana.

DIANA. This is awfully nice cordial, Anne. It's ever so much nicer than my aunt's cordials and she brags of her Josephine ever so much. It doesn't taste a bit like hers. . . . (*DIANA pours a cordial with wild abandon. It spills all over the tablecloth.*)

ANNE. Diana . . . Diana! It's all right, I'll get a cloth. (*DIANA licks up the excess cordial on the table.*) Diana!

DIANA. (*Singing drunkenly.*)
KINDRED SPIRITS . . . JUST YOU AND ME
EVER TO BE . . .

ANNE. Di-ana!!!

DIANA.
LIKE A FLY . . . STICKS TO GLUE
WE'LL STICK TOGETHER JUST ME AND YOU. . . .
I'LL SWEAR AT YOU, YOU SWEAR AT ME.

WE'LL SWEAR AT WE.
NOW WE'RE KINDRED SPIRITS.
(*By now she is drinking straight from the bottle. She tilts back in her chair and pours the cordial down her throat.*)

MRS. BARRY. Di-ana!

DIANA. Oh, h'lo, Mother! (*Giggles.*)

MRS. BARRY. What has happened to my child?

MRS. SPENCER. I think she's squiffy.

MRS. BARRY. I think she's been poisoned!

DIANA. I think I'm going to be sick . . . (*Runs out quickly.*)

ANNE. (*Starting to follow her.*) Don't worry, Mrs. Barry. I'll cope.

MARILLA. Anne! Where did you get this bottle?

ANNE. On the second shelf . . . where you told me. . . .

MARILLA. How much did she drink?

ANNE. Three, maybe four tumblersful. Diana! DIANA! (*She rushes out after her friend.*)

MARILLA. It's my fault. I forgot to bring the cordial up from the root cellar. The child has been drinkin' currant wine.

MRS. PYE. Wine! Why, Marilla Cuthbert, you always said your currant wine wouldn't have the least effect on anybody.

MRS. BARRY. You even gave it to the minister's wife.

MARILLA. Yes, but she didn't drink four tumblersful at a time. However, that's the last of it, you'll be glad to know, and I'd best get rid of it here and now.

(*But* MRS. LYNDE *has firm possession of the bottle. She pours a glassful just to taste. All the other* LADIES *seem to find glasses, too.* MARILLA *won't have to worry about getting rid of it now.*)

ACT TWO

SCENE 5

FLOWER SCRIM AND BLUE SCRIM.

AVONLEA SCHOOL is starting out on a nature hunt.

SONG: *"OPEN THE WINDOW"* (Reprise)

MISS STACY.
LOOK ALL AROUND YOU,
LIFE WILL ASTOUND YOU,

WHY DON'T YOU OPEN UP AND SING?
OPEN THE WINDOW.
NOW WE'LL BEGIN TO
LEARN EVERYTHING!
Now, I want the girls to collect leaves and wild flowers and
there'll be a prize for the one who brings back the most different
kinds. And, boys, let's see who'll be the first to climb a tree and
bring us back an empty bird's nest. Wait! Be careful of the birds
and treat the eggs gently. Now off you go!

(NATURE HUNT BALLET. *The* GIRLS *hunt for butterflies
with nets and only succeed in catching each other. The* BOYS
*manage to catch a frog and in the interests of science, drop
it down* ANNE SHIRLEY'S *back. When she finally retrieves it,*
ANNE *gets revenge on* GILBERT, *the main culprit, by enlisting
the aid of the other boys to slip the frog down his back.*)

MISS STACY.
LOOK ALL AROUND YOU, LIFE WILL ASTOUND YOU.
WHY DON'T YOU OPEN UP AND SING?
OPEN THE WINDOW, NOW WE'LL BEGIN TO
ALL.
LEARN EVERYTHING!

(BOYS *and* GIRLS *exit.* MISS STACY *halts* ANNE *and* GILBERT.)

MISS STACY. Anne Shirley! Gilbert Blythe! Would the two of
you come here please? I have decided to recommend both of you
as candidates for the Avery scholarship. If you accept you will be
competing with students all over the Island, and will also be
competing with each other as there is only one scholarship. It's
worth two hundred and fifty dollars a year for four years at
Queen's College, but it does mean an extra hour's work every
day after school. Are the two of you willing to give up that free
time to try for it? Good! I'm glad. You should be able to help
each other a great deal. . . . (ANNE *and* GILBERT *both turn
away.*) I see.

SONG: *"I'LL SHOW HIM"*
(ANNE *and* GILBERT *in separate spotlights.*)

ANNE.
I'LL SHOW HIM!
I'LL SHOW HIM THAT A GIRL CAN SET HER MIND

TO STUDY HARD AND WORK AND SLAVE AND
    WHEN THE TIME HAS COME HE'LL FIND
I'LL SHOW HIM!
    GILBERT.
THOUGH OTHER BOYS ARE HAVING FUN
BY CLIMBING TREES AND SKIPPING SCHOOL,
    EXCEPT FOR ME, THE ONLY ONE . . .
I'LL SHOW HER!
I KNOW HER!
I KNOW BEHIND THAT FRECKLED FACE
THERE'S JUST A . . . STUCK-UP SNOB WHO ALWAYS
    HAS TO WIN EACH RACE.
    ANNE and GILBERT.
I KNOW HIM (HER)!
    ANNE.
I KNOW THAT GREAT BIG SHOW-OFF BOY
WHO THINKS HE'S OH-SO-EXTRA SMART BECAUSE
    HE'S JOSIE'S PRIDE AND JOY,
I KNOW HIM!
    ANNE and GILBERT.
I'LL COMPETE WITH HIM (HER), MAKE
    MINCEMEAT OF HIM (HER)
AND I NEVER WILL GIVE IN!
NO RETREAT FROM HIM (HER), WIPE THE STREET
    WITH HIM (HER)
YET I KNOW THAT HE (SHE) WILL WIN!
    ANNE.
I KNOW IT!
I KNOW WHAT GILBERT BLYTHE WILL DO!
HE'LL CLOSE HIS BOOKS RIGHT AFTER SCHOOL
    AND NEVER FUSS OR FRET OR STEW.
I KNOW IT!
    GILBERT.
I KNOW THAT WHEN IT COMES THE DAY
I'LL LOSE MY NERVE AND NOT SHOW UP AND
    RUN AWAY!
I'LL THROW IT!
    ANNE and GILBERT.
WON'T COMPETE WITH HIM (HER), I'LL BE BEAT
    BY HIM (HER).
PLEASE JUST FREE ME FROM HIS (HER) GRIP!
I'LL RETREAT FROM HIM (HER), CROW I'LL EAT
    WITH HIM (HER).
HE (SHE) CAN KEEP THE SCHOLARSHIP!

NOOOOOO!

I'LL SHOW HIM (HER)!
I'LL SHOW THAT AWFUL SCHOOLROOM SCAB . . .
  ANNE.
THAT STUCK-UP SNOB!
  GILBERT.
THAT FRECKLED GROUCH!
  ANNE.
THAT TEACHER'S PET!
  GILBERT.
THAT RED-HAIRED CRAB!
  ANNE and GILBERT.
I'LL THROW HIM (HER)!
THE DAY WILL COME WHEN WE WILL WRITE
   THE BIG EXAM . . .
  ANNE.
AND I'LL BE CALM. . . .
  GILBERT.
THE BELL WILL RING AND WHAM!
  ANNE and GILBERT.
I'LL SHOW HIM (HER)!
I'LL SHOW HIM (HER)!

BLACKOUT

ACT TWO

SCENE 6

THE STORE AT CARMODY.

At one side is a headless mannequin displaying a beautiful dress with puffed sleeves. A barrel of pitchforks sits nearby.

  CECIL. Mornin', Earl.
  EARL. Mornin', Cecil.
  CECIL and EARL. Mornin', Lucilla.
  LUCILLA. Why, mornin', Cecil, Earl. What can I do for you?

SONG: *"GENERAL STORE"*

  EARL.
I SEEN A HARNESS . . . 'TWAS OFFERED FOR SALE
IN YER BRAND NEW CATALOGUE.

CECIL.
IT PULLS AT YOUR MOUTH AND FITS UNDER
     YOUR TAIL
AND GIVES YOU A REAL SMART JOG!

LUCILLA. I'll fetch it. . . .

MRS. PYE. G'day.

MRS. BARRY. G'day.

LUCILLA. Good mornin', Mrs. Barry, Minnie. What can I do for you?

MRS. BARRY.
HAVE YOU GOT A GARMENT THAT'S OFFERED
     FOR SALE
IN THE NEW SPRING ALMANAC?

MRS. PYE.
IT TAKES ALL THE FLESH THAT YOU HAVE IN
     THE FRONT
AND MOVES IT AROUND IN BACK!

LUCILLA. That's a cinch! Here, try this on your player piano. (MATTHEW *enters, rattled to find a female clerk.*) Why, Mr. Cuthbert! What can I do for you?

MATTHEW. Well, now, I . . . I . . . is Mr. Blair anywheres about?

LUCILLA. Mr. Blair? Why, no . . . he's gone for the day.

MATTHEW. The day . . . oh, dear!

LUCILLA.
STEP OVER HERE . . . I'M AT YOUR SERVICE.
WHAT CAN I DO FOR YOU?

MATTHEW. Well, I . . . I . . . I . . .

LUCILLA.
PLEASE DON'T BE NERVOUS . . .
I'VE NOTHING ELSE TO DO!

MATTHEW. I want some puff . . . puff . . .

LUCILLA. Puff . . . puff?

CECIL. How's that again, Matthew?

MATTHEW.
I WANT SOME PUFF . . . PUFF . . .

EARL. Pipe tobacco!

LUCILLA.
I'LL WRAP A TIN OF OLD CHUM!

MATTHEW.
NO! I MEAN P . . . P . . . . P . . .

MRS. PYE. Paraffin oil!

LUCILLA.
COMING RIGHT UP . . . ONE DRUM!

(*The* CUSTOMERS *and* LUCILLA, *trying only to be helpful, load* MATTHEW *with all the things the poor fellow is asking for.*)

MATTHEW.
HAVE YOU GOT PUFF . . . PUFF . . .
    CECIL. Paris perfume?
    LUCILLA.
RIGHT NOW WE'RE ALL OUT OF STOCK.
    MATTHEW.
NO, I WANT P . . . P . . . P . . .
    MRS. BARRY. Pickled preserves?
    LUCILLA.
PICKLED PRESERVES! ONE CROCK!

MY ONLY AIM IN LIFE IS BUT TO PLEASE YOU.
A GENERAL STORE IS JUST THE PLACE
TO MEET THE NEEDS OF THE HUMAN RACE . . .
    MATTHEW.
WHAT I REALLY CAME FOR . . .
I REALLY CAN'T SAY.
IT'S MORE LIKE . . . OOPS!
      (MATTHEW *trips over a sack of potatoes.* LUCILLA *thinks he wants it too and enlists the aid of the* MEN *to load it on* MATTHEW's *shoulders.*)
    LUCILLA.
THAT'S ON SPECIAL TODAY!
Cecil, come here and help.
    MATTHEW. (*Sees the dress on the mannequin.*) Ah, oh, oh, now *that's* what I really wanted.
    EARL. Prunes . . .
    MRS. PYE. Pink pills . . .
    CECIL. Peppercorns . . .
    MRS. BARRY. Peaches, pears, plums . . .

(*Heading for the dress,* MATTHEW *stumbles over the pitchforks.*)

    ALL. Pitchforks!
    LUCILLA. At this time of year?

(MATTHEW *reluctantly adds a pitchfork to his purchases.*)

    ALL.
OUR ONLY AIM IN LIFE IS BUT TO PLEASE YOU.
A GENERAL STORE IS JUST THE PLACE
TO MEET THE NEEDS OF THE HUMAN RACE. . . .

LUCILLA. (*Totaling.*)
PUT DOWN SIX AND CARRY TWO.
IS THERE ANYTHING ELSE I CAN DO FOR YOU?

MATTHEW. Rachel! Excuse me, Lucilla. (*Takes* MRS. LYNDE *aside and whispers in her ear.*)

LUCILLA. (*Tallying it all up.*) Now let's see, what have we got here?

MRS. BARRY. Paraffin oil . . .

MRS. PYE. Pipe tobacco . . .

LUCILLA. Pickled preserves . . .

EARL. . . . Peppercorns . . .

CECIL. Potatoes . . .

MRS. LYNDE. The very thing! Puffed sleeves!

LUCILLA. Puffed sleeves?

MATTHEW. Puffed sleeves. (*With determination,* MATTHEW *picks up the dress, mannequin and all, and carts it out of the store.*)

LUCILLA. Hey!

MATTHEW. Charge it!

BLACKOUT

ACT TWO

SCENE 7

ANNE, *standing in a pool of light, is wearing the puffed sleeves.*

DIANA. Anne Shirley, if you aren't the prettiest thing I ever saw!

ANNE. You don't think it makes me look wider, as Marilla said?

DIANA. Oh, no, it makes you look taller. I can hardly wait to see the look on Gilbert Blythe's face.

ANNE. Neither can I.

DIANA. Not to mention Miss Josie Pye.

ANNE. Diana, tonight I have a soul that flies above Josie Pye and everything else.

(*The LIGHTS COME UP and we are in the SCHOOLROOM.
    Frantic preparations are being made for the school concert.*)

GILBERT. (*Entering.*) Diana, can you help me with my lines, please?

DIANA. Of course, Gilbert, but . . .

JOSIE. (*Entering, agitatedly.*) Ohhhh—my mother!

ANNE. Josie, what's the matter?

JOSIE. I told my mother I had to be the spirit of Canada with wings and everything, but she wouldn't lend me her beaded slippers.

ANNE. But your mother's slippers wouldn't have fitted you anyway.

JOSIE. Whoever heard of a fairy in boots with copper toes!— Oh, leave me alone. (*Runs off.*)

(ANNE *ducks behind the curtain of the makeshift stage as* PARENTS *and* FRIENDS *begin to arrive.*)

MRS. LYNDE. Oh, isn't it grand that they got up a concert!

MRS. MACPHERSON. I hear these young people have been practising up for months.

MRS. BARRY. Ohhh, yes. My Diana doesn't mind doing that for a concert. Just try to get her to practise her piano or do her studies and it's a different story.

MRS. LYNDE. I'm sure we're going to be proud of our Diana tonight. Why, Matthew and Marilla, I'm sure we're going to be proud of our Anne tonight. Why, Matthew Cuthbert, you're white as a ghost. What could Dr. Malcolm say?

MARILLA. I'm not surprised, going all the way into Carmody for puffed sleeves and strainin' his valves bringing home a drum of paraffin oil we don't need, a hundred pounds of potatoes I'll never use in a month of Sundays, and enough pitchforks for a threshing gang.

MRS. LYNDE. I know . . . wasn't that a caution!

MATTHEW. Well! I figure it was worth it.

MRS. LYNDE. Why, Mr. Phillips and Prissy . . . I should say Mrs. Phillips . . . I'm sure we're going to be proud of our . . . (MRS. LYNDE *stops short. The new* MRS. PHILLIPS *is considerably pregnant. The* ADULTS *sit at the children's desks.* MRS. PHILLIPS *has difficulty until her husband raises the cover of the desk for her.*) Isn't it grand they got up a concert!

MISS STACY. Ladies and gentlemen . . . ladies and gen . . . ladies and gentlemen, members of the Board of Trustees, honored guests, parents and friends. Tonight we would like to present a pageant of Canadian history which has been written and devised by the pupils of Avonlea School.

MRS. LYNDE. Did you hear that?

MRS. PYE. Isn't that clever? They wrote all their own history.

MISS STACY. But first to open our program . . . we present a famous tableau. (*Draws aside the curtain to reveal a number of her* Pupils *wearing stovepipe hats and beards.*)

Mrs. MacPherson. Isn't that lovely?

Mrs. Pye. What is it?

Mrs. Lynde. That's the Last Supper.

Miss Stacy. It's an event known to each and every one of us . . . the meeting of the Fathers of Confederation. (Rachel *sniffs.*) And now, our pageant.

Josie. I am the spirit of Canada . . .

Diana. (*Behind the curtain.*) But forty years young.

Josie. What?

All Children. I am the spirit of Canada, but forty years young.

(Josie *is frozen with stage fright.* Anne Shirley *comes out, hands her a little basket with her lines in it.*)

Josie. . . . I am the spirit of Canada, but forty years young. Yet my story goes back to the "Ice Age" from whence our first people sprung! . . . Oh, Anne!!!!!!! (*Exits gratefully.*)

Anne.

During the Ice Age . . . Canada slept . . .

For years she lay . . . her virgin soil undisturbed . . .

Except by the odd Eskimo

With his igloo of ice and snow.

     (*Enter* Moody Spurgeon MacPherson *swathed in fur and* Tillie Boulter *dressed as an igloo.*)

Later the proud red Indian came . . .

     (*Enter* Tommy Sloane.)

By stripping the bark of some silver birch

He made his rude forest home.

     (Gertie Pye *holds two branches aloft.*)

Meanwhile far across the Atlantic Ocean

Men of other nations were searching. . . .

Gold was what they sought. . . . What did they find?

Not gold . . . but . . . a golden land. . . .

Miss Stacy. (*Whispering.*) Now!

(Three Explorers *emerge.* Gilbert [*Viking*], Diana [*French*], *and* Josie [*English*].)

Gilbert.

WE'VE SAILED TO NORTH AMERICA TO SEE . . .

Josie and Diana.

WE'VE SAILED TO NORTH AMERICA TO SEE . . .

GILBERT.
IF THERE'S A LAND THAT'S FIT FOR YOU AND
ME . . .

JOSIE.
IF THERE'S A LAND THAT'S FIT FOR YOU AND
ME. . . .

DIANA.
CAN THERE BE DRY LAND . . . QUITE NEAR?

JOSIE.
HERE IS AN ISLAND . . . RIGHT HERE!!!

GILBERT.
NEVER BEFORE HAVE WE SEEN SUCH A LAND.

JOSIE, DIANA and GILBERT.
WAS IT EVER GRAND!

ALL CHILDREN.
THEY CALL IT . . .

PRINCE EDWARD ISLAND, THE HEART OF THE
WORLD
SET IN THE CROSSROADS OF THE SEA!
ALL OF THE NATIONS HAVE THEIR BANNERS
UNFURLED
NOW THAT THEY KNOW THAT THIS IS THE PLACE
TO BE!

PRINCE EDWARD ISLAND, THE HEART OF THE
WORLD
SET IN THE CROSSROADS OF THE SEA!
ALL OF THE NATIONS HAVE THEIR BANNERS
UNFURLED
NOW THAT THEY KNOW THAT THIS IS THE PLACE
TO BE!

DIANA.
PRINCE ED . . .

ANNE.
Prince Edward Island! So each of them left their mark . . .

TILLIE. Ouch!! (MOODY SPURGEON *must have stepped on her
fingers or toes.*)

ANNE.
So each of them left their mark . . .
On this island of ours, this earth,
This realm, this precious jewel
Set in a silver gulf. . . .

(*The* STATIONMASTER *enters waving a telegram.* MRS. LYNDE *takes immediate charge and reads it.*)

ALL CHILDREN.
PRINCE EDWARD ISLAND, THE HEART OF THE
    WORLD
SET IN THE CROSSROADS OF THE SEA!
ALL OF THE NATIONS HAVE THEIR BANNERS
    UNFURLED
NOW THAT THEY KNOW THAT THIS IS THE
    PLACE TO BE!
THEY CALL IT PRINCE EDWARD ISLAND. . . .
    MRS. LYNDE. (*Screams.*) Oh! Oh! Marilla! Look here! Look! Look! (MRS. LYNDE *shows it to her.* MARILLA *takes it proudly to* MISS STACY.)
    MISS STACY. Ladies and gentlemen . . . the winner of the Avery Scholarship . . . is from Avonlea School . . . Miss Anne Shirley! (MATTHEW *clutches his chest. No one notices as* MARILLA *helps him out of the schoolroom.*) And the runner-up, also from Avonlea School . . . Mr. Gilbert Blythe!
    CHARLIE. Hurrah for Anne Shirley and Gilbert Blythe!
    MISS STACY. We are indeed doubly proud of our local boy and girl.
    GILBERT. Congratulations, Anne.
    ANNE. Gilbert, I hope . . . (*Extends her hand in friendship, but* GILBERT, *unable to bear the disappointment, turns away.*)
    DIANA. Hurray for Anne Shirley, the cleverest girl on the Island!
    ALL CHILDREN. Hurray for Anne Shirley!
    MRS. LYNDE. Fellow citizens, it makes me very humble when I think of the small contribution I have made toward this great moment. . . . I feel that . . .
    STATIONMASTER. You? What about me? I seen her first! If it hadn't been for me, she wouldn't be here tonight!

SONG: *"IF IT HADN'T BEEN FOR ME"*

STATIONMASTER.
WHEN I FOUND HER SHE WAS WAITIN'
AT THE STATION DOOR,
DIDN'T HAVE A TAG DESCRIBING
JUST WHERE SHE WAS HEADED FOR,
SHE'D HAVE GONE BACK C.O.D.
IF IT HADN'T BEEN FOR ME!
    ALL.
IF IT HADN'T BEEN FOR YOU,

ALL.
IF IT HADN'T BEEN FOR ME,
IF IT HADN'T BEEN FOR ALL OF US
I WONDER WHERE SHE'D BE?
WHY, WE WOULDN'T HAVE ALL THIS FUSS
IF IT HADN'T BEEN FOR US!
MRS. LYNDE.
WELL, I TOOK A FANCY TO HER
FROM THE VERY START.
SHE WAS SO POLITE AND BASHFUL
THAT SHE WON MY VERY HEART
AND I'M GLAD THAT ALL THOSE BOOKS
HAVEN'T SPOILED THE BEAUTY OF HER LOOKS!

ALL.
IF IT HADN'T BEEN FOR YOU,
IF IT HADN'T BEEN FOR ME,
IF IT HADN'T BEEN FOR ALL OF US
I WONDER WHERE SHE'D BE?
WHY, WE WOULDN'T HAVE ALL THIS FUSS
IF IT HADN'T BEEN FOR US!
MR. PHILLIPS.
IT WAS DESTINY THAT CHOSE ME
TO CULTIVATE THIS PEARL
BY DEVOTING MY ATTENTION
TO THE NEEDS OF EVERY GIRL
FOR IN THE FIELD OF KNOWLEDGE
WHEN YOU PLANT A TINY SEED
THE RESULTS CAN BE TREMENDOUS,
TREMENDOUS, YES, INDEED.
ALL.
IF IT HADN'T BEEN FOR YOU,
IF IT HADN'T BEEN FOR ME,
IF IT HADN'T BEEN FOR ALL OF US
I WONDER WHERE SHE'D BE?
WHY, WE WOULDN'T HAVE ALL THIS FUSS
IF IT HADN'T BEEN FOR US!
     (*DANCE.*)
IF IT HADN'T BEEN FOR YOU,
IF IT HADN'T BEEN FOR ME,
IF IT HADN'T BEEN FOR . . .
MISS STACY. (*Sweetly admonishing them.*) Anne! . . . If it
hadn't been for Anne. She did it herself, with imagination
and determination, and though we may all have helped when we
could, it was Anne who brought honor this night to our school.
. . . So . . .

MISS STACY.
IF IT HADN'T BEEN FOR YOU,
IF IT HADN'T BEEN FOR ME,
I'VE A HUNCH SHE'D STILL HAVE MADE IT
AS THE PRIDE OF AVONLEA.
    GILBERT. (*Coming forward to take* ANNE'S *hand.*)
SHE'S THE GIRL AT THE HEAD OF THE CROWD,
AND I'M FEELING MIGHTY, MIGHTY PROUD.
    ALL.
FEELING MIGHTY, MIGHTY,
OH SO HIGH AND MIGHTY,
FEELING MIGHTY PROUD!

ACT TWO

SCENE 8

FLOWER SCRIM.

BOYS *and* GIRLS *stroll home from the concert, arm-in-arm.*

    SONG: *"THERE IS A GOLDEN SUMMER"*
    TUNE: (*WHY AIN'T IT ALWAYS SUMMER.*)

    CHORUS.
THERE IS A GOLDEN SUMMER
WAITING FOR YOU,
SPINNING A DREAM BY SUNSET
TILL IT COMES TRUE.

(*ORCHESTRA: few bars of "KINDRED SPIRITS,"* ANNE
    and DIANA *arm-in-arm.* TOMMY SLOANE *waits, takes* DIANA
    with him, leaving ANNE *alone.* GILBERT, *a few paces behind,*
    tentatively approaches ANNE.)

    GILBERT.
WONDRIN',
ALL AT ONCE I'M WONDRIN'
WHAT IT'S LIKE TO GROW UP
AND HAVE SOMEONE SHOW UP . . .

        (ANNE *walks off,* GILBERT *follows.*)

    CHORUS.
THERE IS A GOLDEN SUMMER
WAITING FOR YOU,

SPINNING A DREAM BY SUNSET
TILL IT COMES TRUE. . . .

ACT TWO

SCENE 9

KITCHEN, GREEN GABLES.

MATTHEW *is slumped in the rocking chair.* MARILLA *unbuttons his collar.*

MARILLA. I knew we needed an extra hand to help with the heavy work. The doctor said you couldn't do it yourself and now . . .

MATTHEW. Please, Marilla, not now . . .

MARILLA. All that liftin' you been doin', and trottin' into town for puffed sleeves . . . now don't you budge till the doctor gets here. I'm going to try and find the sal volatile in case you get dizzy again. I know I left it somewhere. (*Hurries off.*)

DIANA. (*Off.*) Good night, Anne.

ANNE. Good night. (MATTHEW *makes an effort to straighten up in the chair.* ANNE *comes in, radiant.*) Matthew! I couldn't find you or Marilla anywhere. So we walked home, and we sang all the way . . . and the blossoms looked so white at night . . . and . . . Is anything wrong, Matthew?

MATTHEW. Just bursting proud . . . of my little girl. That's all.

ANNE. And do you know what I kept thinking, all the way home, Matthew? About the first time I saw Green Gables . . . I was in the buggy with you . . . and I talked all the way from the station. Remember? Oh, Matthew, I'm so glad you let me · stay, even though I wasn't a boy.

MATTHEW. We'd rather have had you than a dozen boys. I guess it wasn't a boy who won the Avery scholarship.

ANNE. No, it wasn't . . . but of course Gilbert was runner-up and that's about the same thing. Except . . . without the scholarship his father can't afford to send him to Queen's.

MATTHEW. Gilbert will make his mark, never fear.

ANNE. You know, I think the best thing about winning a scholarship is that it announces to all the world that you've got some sense. I was never sure before, but I think my chances of becoming sensible are greater than ever. Marilla always said I was too romantic by far.

MATTHEW. Don't lose all your romance, Anne. A little romance is a good thing. Keep just a little of it.

SONG: *"ANNE OF GREEN GABLES"*

ANNE OF GREEN GABLES, NEVER CHANGE,
I LIKE YOU JUST THIS WAY,
ANNE OF GREEN GABLES, SWEET AND STRANGE,
STAY AS YOU ARE TODAY.

THOUGH BLOSSOMS FADE AND FRIENDS MUST
　　PART
OLD GROW THE SONGS WE'VE SUNG.
ANNE OF GREEN GABLES, IN MY HEART
YOU ARE FOREVER YOUNG.

(MATTHEW *gasps the last word.*)

ANNE. Matthew?

MATTHEW. Tell Marilla . . . never mind the sal volatile.

ANNE. Sal volatile?

MATTHEW. That's right, dear . . . now run along. Hurry!

ANNE. (*Runs out unaware of what's going on.*) Marilla . . . Marilla!

(MATTHEW *is alone. Slowly and peacefully his head slumps forward. The LIGHT FADES.*)

ACT TWO

SCENE 10

GREEN GABLES.

MARILLA *and* MRS. LYNDE *enter dressed in mourning.*

MARILLA. I'll fix us a good strong cup of tea.

MRS. LYNDE. (*Looking at the empty rocking chair.*) Well, he lived sixty years but he was never happier than he was during this last one. Oh, Marilla, what will you do without him?

MARILLA. Remember him as best we can. I'll take a slip of that little white rose bush Mother brought over from Scotland and plant it by the grave before we leave.

MRS. LYNDE. Leave? For where?

MARILLA. Anne's going to Queen's. That'll be four years. There's nothing to stay for here. I could sell the place and board somewhere.

MRS. LYNDE. But you wouldn't think of leaving Green Gables!

MARILLA. I don't know what else is to be done. I've thought about it. Things would only get behind worse and worse until nobody would want to buy it. It won't bring much, but it'll be enough for me to live on. . . .

MRS. LYNDE. But sell Green Gables . . .

MARILLA. Kettle's boilin'.

MRS. LYNDE. Oh! Now you listen to me, Marilla Cuthbert. We've been friends since we was girls together, you and Matthew and . . . well, you are Green Gables. Without you around here to . . . (*But* MARILLA *doesn't hear. It's as if she were alone with the rocking chair.*)

MARILLA. Oh, Matthew . . . Matthew. You mustn't think I didn't love her as much as you did. It wasn't easy for me to say things . . . but I loved the both of you just as dear as . . .

SONG: *"THE WORDS"* (Reprise.)

I CAN'T FIND THE WORDS,
CAN'T GET OUT THE PHRASES.
WHEN HE NEEDED LOVE
DID I SING HIS PRAISES?

WHERE DID THE WORDS GO
WHEN I WAS BESIDE HIM?
WHY COULDN'T I SHOW
ALL THE LOVE THAT MY HEART
FELT TOWARD HIM?
I ADORED HIM.
    (*Spoken.*)
God reward him. (*Sings.*)
I CAN'T FIND THE WORDS.

MRS. LYNDE. Oh, Marilla, are you all right? Oh, Marilla, was it something I said? (*But* MARILLA *is lost in her thoughts.* ANNE *enters, exchanges a sympathetic look with* MRS. LYNDE *who exits quietly.*)

ANNE. (*Goes to the table and sits.*) I'll have a cup of tea, too, thank you.

MARILLA. (*Startled.*) You near scared me out of my growth. Where did you skip off to?

ANNE. Over to Barrys'.

MARILLA. I thought Diana was over to her Aunt Josephine's for the day.

ANNE. I went to see her father. He's offered to rent the land here at Green Gables, and we can stay in the house just the same.

MARILLA. We? Who's we?

ANNE. You and I. I'm not going to Queen's.

MARILLA. But I can't let you . . . you mustn't give up . . . what about the scholarship?

ANNE. I met Miss Stacy up the road, and talked to her about giving it to someone else . . . only that's not allowed. But she says I can stay here at home and study everything that I would at Queen's.

MARILLA. But four years, Anne!

ANNE. Nothing would be worse than giving up Green Gables.

MARILLA. I can't let you sacrifice yourself like this.

ANNE. I've quite made up my mind, Marilla. Besides, Rachel Lynde says . . . she says, I've enough education as a woman'd be comfortable with. . . .

MARILLA. Anne Shirley . . . (*Embraces* ANNE.)

(GILBERT's *voice is heard off.*)

GILBERT. Anne Shirley! (*Enters the kitchen.*) I wish to speak with you, Anne Shirley. Miss Stacy told me what you tried to do for me, Anne. It was . . . awfully good of you.

ANNE. It wasn't particularly good of me at all, Gilbert. I couldn't go to Queen's and so I saw no reason why somebody . . . well, anybody else shouldn't go.

GILBERT. Anne. You are going to keep up your studies, aren't you?

ANNE. I hope to.

GILBERT. So am I. Well. (*There is a pause.* GILBERT, *embarrassed now, rushes out.*)

ANNE. (*Rushing out the door after him. Catches up with him on the back porch.*) Gilbert!

GILBERT. Maybe this time you'll help me.

ANNE. Gilbert . . . we are going to be good friends, aren't we?

GILBERT. I don't see why not. We've been good enemies. (*They clasp hands in friendship.*)

SONG: *"WONDRIN' "* (Reprise.)

ANNE and GILBERT.
WONDRIN'
WHY WE CAN'T BE SWEETHEARTS
AND WONDRIN'
WHY MY HEART KEEPS THUNDRIN'

WHEN I HOPE YOU'RE WONDRIN'
ABOUT ME THIS WAY.

(GILBERT *leaves happily.* ANNE, *with a shy smile, turns, goes
back into the kitchen, rejoins* MARILLA *at the table. There
is a look of understanding between them.*)

CURTAIN

CURTAIN CALL REPRISE

SONG: *"ICE CREAM"*

ICE CREAM!
IS ANYTHING MORE DELECTABLE
THAN ICE CREAM?
WHY, EVEN THE MOST RESPECTABLE
EAT ICE CREAM.
IT'S WONDERFUL ON A SUMMER'S AFTERNOON
IN JUNE.
ICE CREAM.

COSTUME PLOT

MARILLA:
Act One, Scene 1:
  Dark blue gabardine skirt, with light blue floral print blouse, beige fringed shawl, purse. Black stockings, white gloves, black boot shoes, beige straw hat, gray wig.
Act One, Scene 3:
  Same—less shawl, purse, hat; plus white apron.
Act One, Scenes 4, 5:
  Same—less apron; plus purse, hat, navy cape, gloves.
Act One, Scene 7:
  Same—then take off hat, purse, cape and put on apron in scene.
Act One, Scene 8:
  Same.
Act One, Scene 12:
  Same—plus hat, black cape, gloves.
Act Two, Scene 3:
  Same as Act One, Scene 3.
Act Two, Scene 4:
  Same—but change to green and pink print blouse.
Act Two, Scenes 7, 9:
  Same—but add hat, purse, gloves.
Act Two, Scene 10:
  Black dress, purse, with black stockings, black gloves, black hat and black wig. (Add white apron in scene.)

ANNE:
Act One, Scene 2:
  Gray striped dress with camisole, black tights, black hat, black shoes, red pigtail wig.
Act One, Scene 3:
  Change to blue nightgown in scene, black tights.
Act One, Scene 5:
  Gray striped dress, black tights, black shoes, red pigtail wig.
Act One, Scene 7:
  Gray striped dress, black tights, black hat (takes off), black shoes, red pigtail wig.
Act One, Scenes 8, 9, 10:
  Gray striped dress, add white pinafore, black tights, black shoes, red pigtail wig.

76

Act One, Scene 12:
Gray striped dress, add white pinafore, black tights, flower crown, black shoes, red pigtail wig.

Act One, Scene 13:
Gray striped dress, (remove pinafore?), black tights, black shoes, red pigtail wig.

Act Two, Scene 1:
Gray striped dress, (remove pinafore?), black tights, black shoes, red pigtail wig.

Act Two, Scene 2:
Gray striped dress, (remove pinafore?) black tights, black shoes, red pigtail wig.

Act Two, Scene 3:
Gray striped dress, black tights, black shoes, red pigtail wig.

Act Two, Scene 4:
Green dress with beige lace trim, black tights, green sash, black shoes, short red wig.

Act Two, Scene 5:
Green dress with beige lace trim, black tights, green sash, black shoes, short red wig.

Act Two, Scenes 7, 8, 9:
White eyelet dress and blue satin sash, black tights, pink bow, black shoes, short red wig.

Act Two, Scene 10:
Black dress, black tights, gray gloves, black hat (No. 2), black shoes, short red wig.

Mrs. Lynde:
Act One, Scene 1:
Red paisley blouse with lace insert, brown skirt, orange taffeta cape, yellow parasol, black stockings, black gloves, beige straw with orange and rust and black trim, feathers and flowers hat, black shoes, mouse brown wig.

Act One, Scene 7:
Same—no cape or parasol.

Act One, Scenes 11, 13:
Same?

Act Two, Scene 4:
Same?

Act Two, Scenes 6, 7:
Maroon 2 piece suit, black purse, beige print blouse with lace jabot, black stockings, black gloves, beige straw hat, brown and yellow feathers, black shoes, mouse brown wig.

Act Two, Scene 10:
Black dress with beige lace trim, black purse, black hat.

Mrs. Spencer:

Act One, Scene 1:

Green jacket and skirt, yellow blouse, green parasol, dark gray handbag, petticoat, black tights, black shoes, gray gloves, blue straw hat with dark blue feathers, brown wig.

Act One, Scenes 4, 5, 6:

Purple cotton print blouse. Black, brown, white check jacket and skirt, petticoat, black tights, black shoes, brown gloves, pale felt hat with black band and orange taffeta ribbon trim, brown wig.

Act One, Scene 13:

(?)

Act Two, Scenes 4, 6, 7:

Same as Act One, Scene 4.

Mrs. Barry:

Act One, Scenes 1, 6, 8:

Mauve flowered print dress with mauve lace trim, blue fitted velvet jacket with lace trim, mauve parasol, petticoat, black tights, black shoes, white gloves, beige straw hat trimmed with blue roses and blue velvet bows, brown wig.

Act One, Scenes 11, 12, 13:

Turquoise cotton dress, lace and mauve trim, purple drawstring bag, petticoat, black tights, black shoes, white straw hat with white, purple, turquoise flower and feather trim, brown wig.

Act Two, Scenes 4, 6, 7:

Same as Act One, Scenes 1, 6, 8. Drawstring bag.

Mrs. Pye:

Act One, Scenes 1, 6, 11:

Gray organza pleated blouse with lace trim, gray drawstring bag, beige parasol, petticoat, black shoes, gray gloves, gray straw hat with yellow velvet trim and flowers, auburn wig.

Act One, Scene 13:

Change to green print blouse, green hat, yellow trim.

Back to Act One, Scene 1.

Act Two, Scenes 4, 6:

Yellow cotton print dress and jacket with gray velvet trim.

Act Two, Scene 7:

Same—add gray cape.

Mrs. MacPherson:

Act One, Scenes 1, 6:

Gray and black velvet-collar jacket, gray skirt, pleated inserts, green cotton print blouse, black parasol, petticoat, black stockings, black shoes, black gloves, gray hat with black edging and black and rust trim, dark brown wig.

Act Two, Scenes 11, 13:
Yellow paisley blouse and brown velvet skirt, petticoat, black stockings, black shoes, reddish wig.

Act Two, Scene 6:
Yellow paisley blouse and brown velvet skirt.

Act Two, Scene 7:
Add short green cloak and drawstring bag, green hat.

MRS. BLEWETT:
Act One, Scene 5:
Blue and black striped blouse, black skirt, gray check apron, mouse messy blonde wig.

MISS STACY:
Act Two, Scene 2:
Gray blouse with white trim, gray pleated wool skirt, black stockings, black shoes.

Act Two, Scene 5:
Blue gym bloomers and top, black tights, black shoes.

Act Two, Scene 7:
Same as Act Two, Scene 2—but blue blouse.

GILBERT:
Act One, Scenes 9, 10, 12:
Blue and white striped shirt, red tie, braces, green sleeveless cardigan, brown knee-length pants, green tights, black boots.

Act One, Scene 13:
Same as Scene 9.

Act Two, Scenes 1, 2, 5:
Same—2nd set black boots for shoe dance.

Act Two, Scenes 7, 8:
Brown plaid double-breasted suit, red tie, blue and white shirt, black stockings.

Act Two, Scene 10:
Black suit, white shirt, black tie, black stockings, black boots.

MATTHEW:
Act One, Scenes 2, 3, 4:
Black "Sunday suit," black tie, white shirt, black stockings, black boots, black homburg, gray moustache, gray wig.

Act One, Scenes 7, 12:
Blue overalls, pink undershirt, neckerchief, black stockings, black boots No. 2 (broken on), farmer straw hat.

Act Two, Scene 3:
Blue overalls, pink undershirt, neckerchief, black stockings, black boots No. 2 (broken down), farmer straw hat.
Act Two, Scenes 6, 7, 9:
Same as Act One, Scene 2 (no hat in Act Two, Scenes 7, 9).

MINISTER:
Act One, Scene 1, Act Two, Scene 7:
Black clergy suit, 3 pieces, clerical collar, white stockings, black shoes, homburg hat (Scene 1 only).
Act One, Scene 13:
Same—add boater hat.

MR. PHILLIPS:
Act One, Scenes 9, 10, Act Two, Scene 7:
Black suit, gray tie, white shirt, black stockings, black boots.
Act One, Scene 13:
Red and white striped jacket; white trousers, black tie, white stockings, white shoes, boater hat.

MAILMAN:
Act One, Scenes 1, 6:
Navy twill uniform, black stockings, black boots, uniform cap.

STATIONMASTER:
Act One, Scenes 11, 13:
Blue shirt, suspenders.
Act Two, Scene 6:
Same.
Act Two, Scene 7:
Take off jacket, add visor, sleeve protectors.

FARMER:
Act One, Scenes 1, 11, 13, Act Two, Scenes 6, 7:
Blue overalls, red shirt, gray stockings, black boots, straw hat.

DIANA:
Act One, Scenes 8, 9, 10, 12:
Blue gingham dress with lace insert and trim, blue hairbow, blue apron, petticoat, black tights, black boots.
Act One, Scene 13:
As Act Two, Scene 7 below.
Act Two, Scenes 1, 2:
(?) As Act One, Scene 8.

Act Two, Scene 4:
As Act One, Scene 8—add blue jacket, less apron, black tights, black boots, straw hat with turquoise flowers and bows.
Act Two, Scene 5:
As Act One, Scene 8—remove blue jacket, put on apron.
Act Two, Scenes 7, 8:
Pink and white striped blouse, yellow hairbow, blue and yellow cotton jumper with white lace trim.

JOSIE:
Brown and white checked dress, white trim, yellow plaid pinafore with brown velvet trim, white bloomers, orange hairbow, petticoat, green tights, black boots.

TILLIE:
Green and pink dress with pink inset, white pinafore and bloomers, black hairbow, petticoat, black tights, black boots.

GERTIE:
Red, pink, navy striped dress, lace trim, white bloomers, purple hairbows, petticoat, red stockings, black boots.

RUBY:
Brown dress with black cord trim, blue and white striped pinafore, white bloomers, green hair ribbons, petticoat, black boots, black tights.

PRISSY:
Act One, Scenes 9, 10, 13:
Pink cotton and net, white lace trim and black velvet details, turquoise and white pinafore, pink hairbow, petticoat, black boots, black tights, blonde ringlets.
Act Two, Scene 7:
Add brown cape, tummy pad, brown gloves.

MOODY:
Act One, Scenes 9, 10, 13, Act Two, Scenes 1, 2, 5:
Brown velvet suit, black tie, white shirt, mauve tights, black boots, 2nd pair for shoe dance.
Act Two, Scenes 7, 8:
Gray tweed suit, yellow tie, blue shirt, mauve tights, black boots.

GERRY:
Act One, Scenes 9, 10, 13, Act Two, Scenes 1, 2, 5:
Green check trousers, red neckerchief, navy and white polka dot shirt, black tights, black boots, 2nd pair for shoe dance.

Act Two, Scenes 7, 8:
  Tweed suit, black tie, blue shirt, turquoise tights, black boots.

CHARLIE:
Act Two, Scenes 9, 10, 13, Act Two, Scenes 1, 2, 5:
  Green trousers, light blue tie, yellow print shirt, rust tights, black boots, 2nd pair for shoe dance.
Act Two, Scenes 7, 8:
  Green suit, gold stripe tie, light blue shirt, purple tights, black boots.

MALCOLM:
Act One, Scenes 9, 10, 13, Act Two, Scenes 1, 2, 5:
  Brown trousers, black tie, red and white shirt, red stockings, black boots, 2nd pair for shoe dance.
Act Two, Scenes 7, 8:
  Brown trousers, add gray cardigan, orange tie, white shirt, red stocking, black boots.

TOMMY:
Act One, Scenes 9, 10, 13, Act Two, Scenes 1, 2, 5:
  Maroon cord pants, green suspenders, blue tie, pink and white shirt, yellow stockings, black boots, 2nd pair for shoe dance.
Act Two, Scenes 7, 8:
  Brown suit, blue tie, pink and white shirt, yellow stockings, black boots.

PROP LIST BY SCENE
ACT ONE

Scene 1: FLOWER SCRIM
* 5 parasols
* 1 bible

Scene 2: STATION AND BUGGY
  1 buggy and winch
  1 blue pillow on buggy seat
* 1 traveling bag with board in base to sit on
* 1 blue nightgrown in bag
* 1 pipe, watch, chain, for Matthew

Scene 3: GREEN GABLES
  1 kitchen table (Used in Scene 7, 3, 9.)
  1 rocking chair (Used in Scene 7, 3, 9.)
  1 hutch unit (Used in Scene 7, 3, 9.)
  1 plate rack over hutch (Used in Scene 7, 3, 9.)
  1 stove (Used in Scene 7, 3, 9.)
  1 stovepipe (Used in Scene 7, 3, 9.)
  1 woodbox (Used in Scene 7, 3, 9.)
  1 clotheshook board (Used in Scene 7, 3, 9.)
  1 traveling bag (First used in Scene 2.)
  1 blue nightgown in bag (First used in Scene 2.)
  3 kitchen chairs
* 1 platter with 2 chops, 2 sausages on stove
* 1 bowl of 7 potatoes on stove
* 1 teapot with 2 cups of tea on stove
* 1 cast iron kettle on stove
* 1 box matches on sideboard
* 1 candleholder and candle on sideboard
* 1 dishcloth on sideboard
* 1 dustpan on woodbox
  1 broom
* 1 apron with note in pocket, on middle hook
* 1 tablecloth on table (green)
* 3 plates
* 3 sets cutlery

N.B.: (1) indicates Act One, Scene 1; (*1*) indicates Act Two, Scene 1.
A scene number after the description indicates the first scene used.
An asterisk * indicates prop necessary for rehearsal.

* 2 cups and saucers
* 1 serving fork and spoon
* 1 electric practical lantern

    1 bed unit (Used in Scene 7, 3.)
    1 skirt and mattress (Used in Scene 7, 3.)
    1 patchwork quilt (Used in Scene 7, 3.)
    1 pillow (Used in Scene 7, 3.)
    1 pair print curtains (Used in Scene 7, 3.)
    1 pair lace curtains (Used in Scene 7, 3.)
    1 night table (Used in Scene 7, 3.)
    1 lace cover (Used in Scene 7, 3.)
    1 box matches on night table (Used in Scene 7, 3.)
    1 dresser (Used in Scene 7, 3.)
    1 mirror frame (Used in Scene 7, 3.)
    1 box matches on dresser (Used in Scene 7, 3.)

Scenes 4 and 5: PATCHWORK AND BLEWETT
* 1 soft straw shopping basket (Mrs. Spencer)
* 1 pad and stub pencil
* 1 paper document "facts"
    2 laundry assemblies for hanging
    3 Blewett chairs
    1 stove on dolly
    1 pot with rubber insert on stove
    1 wooden spoon in pot
    1 cast iron iron on stove
    1 Blewett table
    1 Blewett box
    1 crib with bedding inside
    1 laundry basket full of laundry
* 1 blue blanket on table
* 1 blue blanket set on laundry batten
    1 frying pan

Scene 6: PATCHWORK
    1 hoe
* 1 mailman's bag
* 1 brown bottle in bag
    4 parasols (number ?) (First used in Scene 1.)
    1 soft straw shopping basket (First used in Scene 4, 5.)

Scene 7: GREEN GABLES
All Green Gables props in Scene 3 with postscript (7)
    3 kitchen chairs (First used in Scene 3.)
    1 tablecloth (First used in Scene 3.)

* 1 sewing basket with fabric samples
* 2 plates on sideboard (First used in Scene 3.)
* 2 cups and saucers on sideboard (First used in Scene 3.)
* 1 dishcloth on sideboard (First used in Scene 3.)
* 1 dustpan (First used in Scene 3.)
  1 broom (First used in Scene 3.)
* 1 iron kettle (First used in Scene 3.)
* 1 apron with note in pocket (? used here?) (First used in Scene 3.)
* 1 teapot (First used in Scene 3.)
* 1 bucket of eggs
* 1 bundle of firewood
  1 ladder approximately 10' long

Scene 8: GREEN GABLES
   1 note for Anne in Marilla's apron (First used in 3, 7.)
Scene 9, 10 School
   School desk unit
   Blackboard with flagpole and flag
   Eraser on blackboard
 * Pointer on blackboard
   Teacher's table
 * Slates (12) in desks
 * Chalk (12 pieces) in desks
 * 1 breakaway slate
 * Notes for Gilbert in desk
 * Anne's note for Mr. Phillips (First used in Scene 3, 7, 8.)
 * Pitch pipe for Mr. Phillips
 * Prunes
 * 4 skipping ropes
 * 14 sets foam-filled books with straps
 * 1 soccer ball
   Bicycle
 * Slingshot
 * Teacher's bell

Scene 11: DID YOU HEAR?
   * 1 brown-paper-wrapped parcel
     1 apron (Josie?)
     1 telephone on back of R. portal with flipper
     1 store counter dolly with phone receiver under

Scene 12: FLOWER SCRIM
   1 hoe for Matthew
   1 daisy crown for Anne (?)

Scene 13: CROSSOVER AND PICNIC
* * 1 mailbag containing bottle and 1 leg tie
* * 12 leg ties (or more?)
* * 13 eggs and spoons
* * 1 loose egg and spoon
* 1 picnic table (Belinda table)
* * 8 picnic baskets
* * 2 plates of cookies
* * 1 blue tablecloth
* * 1 race ribbon
* 1 picnic table with red cloth
* * 21 cones
* Holder for cones under picnic table
* * 1 ice cream bucket and mounting prong on table
* * Wooden spoon for bucket
* * Starter pistol for Minister
* * 1 gray straw-flecked blanket and loose straw
* * 1 trick cone for Gilbert

ACT TWO

Scenes 1 and 2: FENCE AND SCHOOL
* * (   ) sets schoolbooks (First used in Scene 10.)
* 1 fence unit
* * (   ) skipping ropes (First used in Scene 10.)
* 2 soccer balls (First used in Scene 10.)
* * 5 single flower stems
* 1 hoe (First used in Scene 6.)

Scenes 3 and 4: GREEN GABLES
* All Green Gables props in Act One, Scene 3 with postscript (3)
* 1 tablecloth (First used in Scene 3.)
* 2 kitchen chairs (First used in Scene 3.)
* 1 dustpan (First used in Scene 3.)
* 1 broom (First used in Scene 3.)
* * 1 glass vase
* * 2 green sashes
* * 1 bottle of "dye"
* * 1 green wig
* * 1 short wig (Anne's)
* * 1 pair scissors
* * 1 cream pitcher
* 1 quick-change board

* 1 cordial bottle
* 5 trick glasses
* 1 cake on rack
* 1 pot holder
* 1 hand mirror
* 1 plate of cookies
* 2 starched napkins, 1 with velcro

Scene 5: FLOWER AND PATCH
* 1 frog and pocket for front of stage
* 1 daisy circle
* 2 fishing rods (??)
* 1 green crow's egg
* 1 butterfly headpiece
* 3 butterfly nets
* 3 bundles leaves
* 1 magnifying glass
* 1 wasp nest on stick
* 1 bird

Scene 6: STORE
Store dolly (First used in Scene 11.)
Paraffin can
Potato sack with string for thumb
Corset
2 almanacs
Crock of preserves
Tin of tobacco
Bill book and pencil
1 keg with weights and bundle of pitchforks
1 5-prong pitchfork
1 puffed sleeve dress on dummy

Scene 7: SCHOOL CONCERT
School desk unit (First used in Scene 9.)
Blackboard unit (First used in Scene 9.)
Teacher's chair
School concert proscenium with curtain
8 black and/or gray coats on desks
8 black hats on desks
1 pair copper-toed shoes
1 telegram
1 wooden mallet
1 parka
2 Indian headbands

2 Indian blankets
1 igloo
1 paisley shawl
1 beige shawl
1 stocking cap
1 large Union Jack
1 laurel headband
1 brown cape
1 green sash
8 beards
1 basket with "prompt" notebook
2 mittens
1 Viking hat
1 3-corned hat
1 musketeer's hat with brown feather
1 Columbus hat (brown cloth, black feather)
Pink shovel bonnet
3 flags
6 small Union Jacks
2 tree branches

Scenes 9, 10: GREEN GABLES
All Green Gables props in Act One, Scene 3 with post-script (*9*)
2 kitchen chairs (First used in Scene 3.)
1 tablecloth (First used in Scene 3.)
1 teapot (First used in Scene 3.)
1 iron kettle (First used in Scene 3.)
2 cups and saucers (First used in Scene 3.)
1 apron on hook (First used in Scene 3.)

GENERAL PROPS:
    Quick change room U. L.
    Lights for carts and quick change (electric, but props to check)
    Prop carts L. and R.
    Music stand, mirror, clothes tree for quick change
    Mirror on Green Gables bed masking flying piece

SUPPLIES:
    * Jar and disinfectant for spoons
    Dream Whip, gelatine, mixing supplies
    Koolaid, instant tea
    Chalk (soft)
    Teacher's pointers
    Blanks for pistol
    Matches, candles
    Prunes

SCENE DESIGNS

The illustrations on page 90 show the complete floor plans for Green Gables. At the bottom is shown the triangular roof piece that flies in to conceal action in the bedroom.

On page 91 are shown the plans for Act One, Scenes 2, 5, and 10.

On page 92 are shown the plans for Act One, Scene 13 and Act Two, Scenes 1, 6, and 7. In the last floor plan (scene 7) is shown the curtained unit stage left where the students hide before their "scenes" come up.

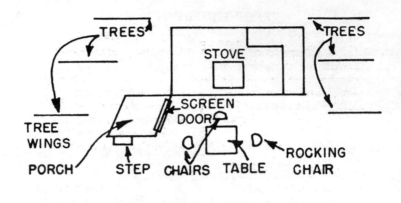

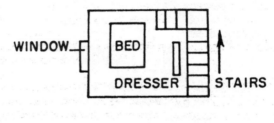

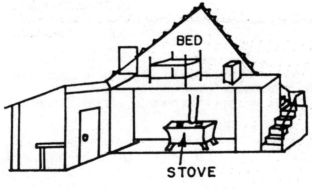

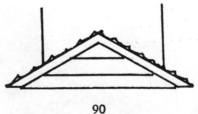

90

TREES

SCRIM

TREE

TREE WINGS

STATION CUTOUT

DROP

BUGGY ←

CRADLE

CHAIRS

TABLE

STOVE

SCHOOL BACKING

BLACK BOARD

DESKS

TABLE

TABLE

SCHOOL BACKING

FENCE

DROP

PILE OF
RAKES

COUNTER

DUMMY WITH
PUFFED SLEEVES

POTATOES

SCHOOL BACKING

DESKS

CURTAINED UNIT

CHAIR

Other Publications for Your Interest

LITTLE SHOP OF HORRORS
(ALL GROUPS—MUSICAL COMEDY)

Book and Lyrics by HOWARD ASHMAN
Music by ALAN MENKEN

5 men, 4 women—Combination Interior/Exterior

Based on the film of the same name by Roger Corman. Screenplay by Charles Griffith. Look Out, here comes Audrey II! Live, and in Living Color, thrill to the excitement as Seymour, lowly assistant to florist Mr. Mushnik, desperately tries to satisfy the voracious craving for human flesh of the unearthly plant which seems to grow before our very eyes, singing and dancing its way into our hearts—literally. Sigh as Seymour tries to win the love of Audrey I (also known as Audrey), who also works in the shop. Her sado-masochistic dentist (isn't that redundant?) boyfriend becomes quite a tasty meal for the plant: but not its last! Suspense! Laughter! Chills! Music! Drama! And, a ''60's Girl-Group'' Chorus! ''Adorable little spoof.''—W.W. Daily. ''Gleefully gruesome. This horticultural horror will have you screaming with laughter.''—N.Y. Post. ''It leaves the audience feeling just like Audrey II between victims—ravenous for more.''—N.Y. Times. This long-running off-Broadway success was originally produced by the excellent W.P.A. Theatre in NYC.

(#666)

A DAY IN HOLLYWOOD/
A NIGHT IN THE UKRAINE
(ADVANCED GROUPS—MUSICAL REVUE)

Book and Lyrics by DICK VOSBURGH
Music by FRANK LAZARUS
Additional Music and Lyrics by Various Composers

4 men, 4 women, 1 pianist on stage, 2 pianists backstage—2 Sets

''Hollywood'' is a marvelous nostalgic spoof of Hollywood and the movies of the 1930s that will delight both those who remember it and those too young to have known it. ''Ukraine'' is the comedy the Marx Brothers didn't make, but could have. It is ever-new, ever-fresh Marx Brothers updated and transformed into comic symbols of their time. This is a ''musical double feature'' and like the old movie double-header there is no connection between the two acts. But together it is fascinatingly successful. ''The puns have wings . . . you leave the theatre with the dizzy feeling of having witnessed a super, impossibly professional senior-class spring show. Not a bed feeling, at all.''—N.Y. Daily News. ''It is crazy, zany magic . . . a smashing show, classy, sassy nostalgia.''—N.Y. Post. ''Act One is a splendidly funny and remarkably clever entertainment, Act Two has inspired lunacy, impeccable foolishness and perfectly hilarious nonsense.''—WCBS-TV2. ''A real winner . . . consists of two extended sketches, both gems.''—Wall Street Journal.

A Day in Hollywood/A Night in The Ukraine (#6658)
A Night in The Ukraine (#16057)

Other Publications for Your Interest

PUMP BOYS AND DINETTES
(ALL GROUPS—MUSICAL)
By JOHN FOLEY, MARK HARDWICK, DEBRA MONK, CASS MORGAN, JOHN SCHIMMEL and JIM WANN

4 men, 2 women—Composite Interior

This delightful little show went from Off Off Broadway to Off Broadway to Broadway, where it had a long run. This is an evening of country/western songs performed by the actors—on guitars, piano, bass and, yes, kitchen utensils. There are the four Pump Boys: L.M. on the Piano (singing such delights as "The Night Dolly Parton Was Almost Mine"), Jim on rhythm guitar (the spokesman of the Pump Boys), Jackson on lead guitar (whose rocker about Mona, a check-out girl at Woolworth's, stops the show) and Eddie, who plays bass. The Dinettes are Prudie and Rhetta Cupp, who run the Double Cupp Diner across from the Pump Boys' gas station. "Totally delightful . . . the easiest, chummiest, happiest show in town."—Newsweek. "Totally terrific."—N.Y. Post. "It tickles the funny bone and makes everybody feel, just for the evening, like a good ole boy or a good ole girl."—Time. "It doesn't merely celebrate the value of friendship and life's simple pleasures, it embodies them."—N.Y. Times. (#18135)

GOLD DUST
(ALL GROUPS—MUSICAL)
Book by JON JORY
Music and Lyrics by JIM WANN

5 men, 3 women, 3 piece combo—Interior

Set in a saloon in a western mining camp in the 1850's, *Gold Dust* is a *very* loose musical adaptation of Molière's *The Miser*. The story concerns a prospector named Jebediah Harp who has hit it rich and hoards his gold. Perfect for high schools, colleges and community theatres, this is another hit from Louisville's famed Actors Theater. The music and lyrics are by the very talented Jim Wann, whose other works include *Pump Boys and Dinettes*, *Diamond Studs* and *Hot Grog*. "It's spunky and raucous, clangorous and tuneful. It overflows with a theatrical zest that is pretty much irresistible."—Louisville Courier Journal. ". . . the small musical that budget-minded theatres across the land have been praying for."—Louisville Times. "Best of all is Wann's music, a mixture of jazz, blues, rock, folk and country-western styles."—Variety. (#9134)

Other Publications for Your Interest

A . . . MY NAME IS ALICE
(LITTLE THEATRE—REVUE)

Conceived by JOAN MICKLIN SILVER
and JULIANNE BOYD

5 women—Bare stage with set pieces

This terrific new show definitely rates an "A"—in fact, an "A-*plus*"! Originally produced by the Women's Project at the American Place Theatre in New York City, "Alice" settled down for a long run at the Village Gate, off Broadway. When you hear the songs, and read the sketches, you'll know why. The music runs the gamut from blues to torch to rock to wistful easy listening. There are hilarious songs, such as "Honeypot" (about a Black blues singer who can only sing about sex euphemistically) and heartbreakingly beautiful numbers such as "I Sure Like the Boys". A . . . *My Name is Alice* is a feminist revue in the best sense. It could charm even the most die-hard male chauvinist. "Delightful . . . the music and lyrics are so sophisticated that they can carry the weight of one-act plays".—NY Times. "Bright, party-time, pick-me-up stuff . . . Bouncy music, witty patter, and a bundle of laughs".—NY Post. (#3647)

I'M GETTING MY ACT TOGETHER AND TAKING IT ON THE ROAD
(ALL GROUPS—MUSICAL)

Book and Lyrics by GRETCHEN CRYER
Music by NANCY FORD

6 men, 4 women—Bare stage

This new musical by the authors of *The Last Sweet Days of Isaac* was a hit at Joseph Papp's Public Theatre and transferred to the Circle-in-the-Square theatre in New York for a successful off-Broadway run. It is about a 40-year-old song writer who wants to make a come-back. The central conflict is between the song writer and her manager. She wants to include feminist material in her act—he wants her to go back to the syrupy-sweet, non-controversial formula which was once successful. "Clearly the most imaginative and melodic score heard in New York all season."—Soho Weekly News. "Brash, funny, very agreeable in its brash and funny way, and moreover, it touches a special emotional chord for our times."—N.Y. Post. (#11025)

ON THE TWENTIETH CENTURY

(ALL GROUPS—MUSICAL COMEDY)

Book and Lyrics by ADOLPH GREEN and BETTY COMDEN, Music by CY COLEMAN

17 principal roles, plus singers and extras (doubling possible)—Various sets

Whether performed with elaborate scenery, or on a simple skeletal scale, this brilliantly comic musical can appeal to audiences everywhere. This is truly an extravagant show—but its extravagance lies not in its scenery and physical production, but in the boisterous, tumultuous energy—and in the lush and sprightly energetic surge of its very melodic score. The story concerns the efforts of a flamboyant theatrical impressario to persuade a film star to appear in his next production, to outwit rival producers and creditors, to rid himself of religious nut Letitia Primrose (played by Imogene Coca on Broadway) and Lily's film star boyfriend Bruce Granit (who's as strong in profile as he is weak in brains). And, he must do all this before the famed 20th Century Ltd. reaches NYC! The story, and it's two leading characters—the mad impressario Oscar Jaffe and the love of his life and his greatest star Lily Garland—can be loved and enjoyed by all audiences. "Spectacular . . . funny . . . elegant . . . civilized wit and wild humor."—N.Y. Times. "A perfect musical . . . a gorgeous show!"—N.Y. Post.   (#819)

KURT VONNEGUT'S GOD BLESS YOU, MR. ROSEWATER

(MUSICAL SATIRE)

By the creators of LITTLE SHOP OF HORRORS

Book and Lyrics by HOWARD ASHMAN
Music by ALAN MENKEN
Additional lyrics by DENNIS GREEN

10 men, 4 women (principals—also double smaller roles), extras, musicians—Various interiors and exteriors

"One of Vonnegut's most affecting and likeable novels becomes an affecting and likable theatrical experience, with more inventiveness, cockeyed characters, high-muzzle-velocity dialogue and just plain energy that you get from the majority of play-wrights."—Newsweek. Eliot Rosewater's a well-intentioned idealist and philanthropic nut—and as president of a multi-million family foundation dispenses money to arcane and artsy-crafty projects. He's also a World War II veteran with a guilt complex, haunted by all this wealth—and also slightly crazy. His outlandish behavior enrages his senator dad, alienates his society-conscious wife—and the money attracts a young, shyster lawyer who tries to divert it to an obscure branch of the family. It portrays Vonnegut's vision of money, avarice and human behavior—as it aims a satrical fusillade at plastic America, fast foods, trademarks, slogans, media blitzes and the follies of materialism. "A charming, delightful, unexpected and thoughtful musical."—N.Y. Post.   (#630)